Fishbowl International, Inc.

SMALL PACKAGES

Sydney Molare'

ISBN: 0-9745188-2-4
Library of Congress Control Number: 2004102030

Printed in the United States of America

First Printing April 2004 by:

Fishbowl International, Inc.
"Viewing Life from all Angles"
PO Box 362
Roxie, MS
www.fishbowlinternational.com

Other Books by Sydney Molare'

Somewhere In America

Changing Faces, Changing Places

This is for the woman in us we always wanted to be…

SMALL PACKAGES

www.sydneymolare.com

Prelude to a Party

Thank God it's Friday!

I slam the door hurriedly, the plastic bags of groceries barely restrained in my arms. Shoving and pushing, I finally manage to get all of them haphazardly onto the countertop. Leaning against the cool granite, I rub my shoulders and the back of my neck which is tight from the strain of the bags, before beginning the boring job of separating and putting the foodstuff in its rightful place.

When are we finally going to reach the Space Age they promised when I was a kid? I mean, by now, we ought to be living like the Jetsons—robot maid, computer delivered food and vacations on Jupiter…media lies. All of it!

I stare at the sun pouring through the bay window of the sunken living room. The waves in the Gulf of Mexico move lazily; the joggers kicking up the sand as they run by. I sigh, wishing I had time to sink onto the fur-lined sofa and relax for a minute. Knowing good and well if I sat down even for a second, I wouldn't get the task at hand finished any time soon. Sluggish hands begin picking at the food.

Whew! Finished.

I hurry down the hallway, my fingers nimbly undoing the buttons of my silk blouse. Eager to shed this outer skin. I never break stride as I let the blouse slide down my arms and drop to the floor. The skirt is next. Just as the zipper reaches its limit, I step out and leave it, a distant cousin to the blouse, on the floor. The bra and panties assume their positions as co-drum majors at the forefront of the clothes parade.

The cool air caresses my nakedness as I walk towards my bedroom. I approach the door with a myriad of emotions—anticipation, longing, need—for behind this previously nondescript door made bold by my own hands, is a sanctuary. A container of nurturing vapor held in place by a flaming red door.

Unable to resist, I push open the door and rush inside. Immediately, I feel a warm bubbling in my stomach. I sigh like I'd just been with an old know-his-way-around-the-bed lover and survey the room. My haven. My soul rejuvenator.

The sun's rays slant through the tall, narrow, stained-glass windows, dust motes playing tag in the light. Bleached pine floors reflect this light onto the large, gaudily ornate mirror placed over an equally ornate fireplace mantle. Huge pillows in every color of the rainbow are scattered around the room. A bed, my bed, covered in resplendent gold satin, is suspended dead center. And of course, the candles. The boucoup candles in every shape and color line the outer walls, the mantle, the window seat and surround the bed. All of them in the same scent—Bridgewater. I inhale the intoxicating fragrance deeply.

My fingers reach eagerly for the matches and I slowly crisscross the room, lighting and coaxing a flame from each stalk of wax. When all are lit, I smile at the scene and roll myself onto the now swaying bed. The movements caress my work-tired mind and slowly, I'm lulled into sleep....

BLEP! BLEP! BLEP!

Huh?!

BLEP! BLEP! BLEP!

"Hello?" I say groggily into the phone.

"Girl, your....*bzzz*...sleep?" A voice I recognize as my friend, Trina, yells into the phone. The intermittent static on the line tells me she is on her cellular.

"No, I'm awake. I must of just dozed off for a minute."

"Well, have you got...*bzzz*....thing for tonight? Do I need to stop...*crackle*...where for some last minute stuff?" I strain to hear her clearly. Today is the day for our Somebody Holler! Book Club sleepover. The four of us—Trina, Travesteen, Cherise and myself— meet monthly to discuss a new book and to hash, trash and ruminate on our favorite subjects—men and sex. We take turns staying over at each other's place one Friday night, spending the first night discussing a book followed by an orgy of shopping on Saturday. It's my turn to play host today.

"No, I have everything. Oh, you know if y'all are planning to drink, it's BYOB."

"We know. Look, I've got Travesteen with me and...*bzzz*...to get off on I-90 to pick up Cherise, so expect us...*bzzz*...next hour. It all depends on whether or not Cherise has her shit...*crackle*... already or not and if this d...*bzzz*...Biloxi traffic lets up."

Chuckling, because we *all* know how slow Cherise is, I tell her, "Great. I'll be waiting on you."

"Hey, you *did* remember to bring the book, didn't you? I don't want to show up there and you don't have jacksh...*bzzz*... to discuss like a couple of months ago." She was referring to the last time I was host of the book club meeting. Somehow my wires got crossed up and I thought one of the other girls was bringing a book to review and they all thought I was the one with the book. Anyhow, we ended up with no book. To say Trina was pissed as hell is an understatement.

"I've got it. I've got it. You just get your tired behinds over here 'cause I'm ready for y'all."

"We'll see. I'll catch ya in an hour or so. By...*crackle*."

I smile as I replace the phone in its cradle. Stretching lazily, I swing my legs over the side of the bed and luxuriate in the rocking motion; refreshed from the miniature catnap. Lifting myself to the floor, I slowly begin extinguishing the candles.

Finished, I pad out of the room—closing the door tightly to avoid the smoke detector sensors—and into my large bathroom. The cool marble floors diminish any sounds but the soft swish of my thighs meeting and separating. Not vain, I ignore my reflection in the floor-to-ceiling mirrors as I continue on to the double shower in the corner. The knobs turn with ease and in milliseconds the warm water is hitting me from all over.

Oh, how I love this shower!

I should. I paid a pretty penny for this baby here. After I saw one like it in Tyrese's video, I knew I had to have one myself.

I let the water sluice all over me until it begins turning cool and reluctantly, I turn it off. After shaking myself like a wet dog—during which time a minimum amount of water is displaced, if any—I grab a thick towel and begin drying myself. Wrapping my hair, I pause in front of the wall of mirrors. Golden skin, dark, inky eyes surrounded by a heavy lid of lashes and full lips stare back at me.

Not so bad, Ms. Zariah Cook. Not so bad at all for a forty year old, never-been-married corporate lawyer, I muse.

Dropping the towel, I turn from side to side, assessing myself for some reason.

You're not going on a date. You're just having your book club girls over, you know, my mind interjects.

I know, but is sure would be nice to actually be going on a date with a man.

You could go on a date. You're just too choosy, it niggles me further.

And I'm gonna stay that way!

Refusing to have a mind argument with my ever-present "Dear Abby" brain cell imitators about my nonexistent love life, I reclaim my towel and walk into my messy dressing room. Stepping over clothes worn from some other time, I grab a pair of men's thigh length briefs—left by a previous flame—and a caftan I picked up at my favorite discount store, Fred's. Pulling everything on, I push my feet into pink footies with matching pompoms on the heel and head back towards the living room.

Chopping and skewering vegetables for our little girl get-together, I chuckle as I think about those three crazy women. How did four totally *different* people form such a close-knit band of friends?

First, we have Trina, my lawyer-in-crime. Big, bold and brash. There was no mistaking you were in the presence of a Queen. A plus-size queen. When I first started working at Delaney's and Company, I thought to myself, this sister has it *all* together—slick suits, tight hair and nails and a domineering attitude. If you didn't know where you stood with her, she definitely wouldn't minch words telling you. She was in charge of something up in there!

I was intimidated by her very presence in a room. But after a few months, she seemed to…mellow. The office gossip was she was in *love*. And you know how a little love will change your *whole* outlook on life. I gave her plenty of room anyhow. She worked divorce and I was in taxes, so our paths rarely crossed.

Then one day, I heard someone crying in the bathroom. Really boohooing. Not sure whether to offer help or ignore the situation, I hurried to finish my business and leave. Unfortunately, my business took more time than I expected and I happened to be exiting my stall just as she was exiting hers.

She looked a mess! Tear tracks had smeared her makeup and some had pooled around the multiple folds of her neck. Offering her some tissues, but reluctant to offer unwanted comfort, I stayed silent as she patted her eyes dry and straightened her clothes. Without a word or a look at me, she began repairing her makeup job. I must tell you, the transformation was an awe-inspiring testimony to the powers of beauty products. When she finished, she turned towards me and said, "Wanna do lunch?"

Still in the clutches of the amazing transformation, I stuttered out a surprised, "Y…yes."

"Let's go then." She leaned towards me. " I'm glad it was you and not one of those nitwits from the outer office. If they'd seen me this way, I can imagine what they would be saying." Her face turned sad. "Unfortunately, they would be right."

"Let me guess. It was a man."

"Ain't it always?" Trina burst out in laughter and I joined her. We ate lunch together and we've continued to eat it together whenever we can.

Now, Travesteen and I met when she was referred to me as a client. She had plenty of money and too many ex-husbands—four, to be exact—who wanted her money. A thirty-eight year old, chicken-farm raised, chocolate Southern Belle, trust-fund girl, Travesteen is a picture of the old south. She still wears a Pillbox hat and white gloves to church! *What decade is this again?* I like to refer to her as Scarlett O'Hara in firecracker pantyhose. I think if a man *breathed* at her right, she was already seeing how his last name fit with hers. I don't know why. It's not like Travesteen goes relatively well with any other name.

Anyway, she was interested in tax shelters which could shield her from this ex or that ex who wanted a piece of her fortune. I knew when I heard her soft drawl which reminded me so vividly of my rural childhood, we were sisterkin. And I was right. We clicked and have been clicking for the past three years. It was a plus to find out Trina had handled her latest divorce. Three peas in a pod.

In fact, it was Travesteen who came up with the idea of the book club. She always had a book in her suitcase handbag—Morrison, Williams, Faulkner, somebody. Both Trina and I were intrigued by the idea so we decided to give it a try.

At first, the going was slow. Travesteen seemed to pick authors with the longest, most complex, read-between-the-lines novels. At one point I considered opting out of the club since most of the "great" fiction had too much usage of the "N" word for me. Still, I trudged along grudgingly, wanting something else, but not sure of what the "something else" was. Travesteen sensed this and suggested the sleepover part followed by shopping to spice up the club a bit. Didn't seem to help much at all. But, all this changed when Cherise joined our group.

Cherise…what can I say? A graduate student in a Marine Physiology Ph.D. program, Cherise is the *slowest* woman in the world. Guinness probably has her listed in its book. If we tell her the meeting starts at seven, she'll make it by eight. And of course, she wants us to rehash what's happened in her absence. It's gotten to the point where we pick her up to ensure she will be there on time.

We met by accident and I do mean *accident*. She managed to run into the back of my brand new, three-day-old Lexus at a stoplight. The only folks at the light were me and her. She was *behind* me and still managed to hit my car.

I hopped out pissed as hell! But, the fat, going-black-fast eye she was sporting along with her torn clothes, made my anger temper and concern surface. Here was this white—*on second glance*—damn-near-white woman trying to conceal her pain while she checked out the damage to my car. Seeing her holding her side and slowly pulling her right leg as she walked around the front of the seen-better-days 1980's Gremlin, I told her to forget the police. I had insurance, so we'd just call it a hit-and-run.

A smile broke through her knuckle-fattened lips and I could see where she was missing part of her left eyetooth. I winced. *Who messed up this chick?*

"I look bad, don't I?" She mumbled, before looking towards the ground.

I couldn't deny the truth. "Yeah. What happened?"

"My girlfriend beat me up."

Girlfriend? Uuuuuhhhhh uh. I just misheard. She must have said boyfriend.

"Well, I'm a lawyer and you know you can get protection from him," I said soothingly, deciding to ignore her apparent misspeak.

"It's not a him, it's a *her*." There was much attitude and emphasis on the 'her'. "My girlfriend. I already called the police…but for some reason, they think domestic violence doesn't apply to lesbians."

I took a step backwards—my homophobia kicking in—as I thought of something else to say. But, what was there to say? Finally, I rummaged around in my purse and pulled out a business card. "I don't know why they haven't done something, but if I can be of service, just let me know."

"You mean that?" Her hazel eye—the good one—lit up and she took a step forward.

Lord, don't let this girl hug me!

"Sure," I answered in relief as she stopped a foot short of me. "Are you going to be all right?"

"I think so. I've just got to find some place else to hide out for a while. I'm a grad student so maybe I can camp out in my office up at school." I saw her pondering this for a moment before reality hit. "Shoot! I won't be able to go in for a few days looking like this though, will I?" She looked at me questioningly.

I shook my head since she definitely looked a sight. Anger, hurt and shame flitted through my body. Here was a woman in need of help and all I want to do was get away from her because she was gay. Just send her back to whatever female monster did this to her.

Where is your sister love, girl? my conscience chided me.

Does sister love apply to lesbians?

Nevertheless, I pushed aside the pros and cons offered by opposing sides in my mental debate and hesitantly offered to let her sleep on my couch until she could find somewhere else to go.

I know, I know. In this day and age you can't offer to let just anybody sleep on your couch. And definitely not in the upscale neighborhood where I lived at the time. It's asking for trouble. But, something told me this girl had too much trouble of her own to try to give me some. I mean, the limp might be fake—*I* didn't think so—but the fat lip, broken tooth and purpling eye definitely weren't. So, I ignored my reservations, hid my shameful homophobia and offered. She accepted and lived there a month until she found other housing.

I took plenty of ribbing from Travesteen and Trina, especially, about aiding-and-abetting a lesbian. But, I didn't care. As long as she didn't come crawling into my bed, we were cool. I locked the door anyway, just in case. *I'm not trying to help nobody get to Hell any sooner than necessary.*

Cherise was still sleeping on my couch when we held a book club meeting at my apartment. After listening for a while, she suggested we read something more contemporary, relative to us. In fact, she pulled out a copy of her latest novel—Omar Tyree's *Just Say No.* I fell in love with African American authors right then and there. Did I holla? I think we all did. No more dry Eudora Welty or Hemingway for us. We needed the grittier writing styles and story lines which connected with us. Our experiences.

We asked Cherise to join right away and she fit into the group like an expensive pair of shoes. Oh, she is a still little on edge whenever we meet since Trina always has plenty of lesbo/dyke/bulldagger comments directed at her, but I smooth things over as best as I can and we seem to have a good time.

Me? Well, I tend to be the peacekeeper, the Sergeant at Arms. I like to keep the arguments to a minimum. Keep the rhythm of the book going. It tough, though…

The sound of a car screeching in the driveway breaks my rehashing of memories. Walking quickly, I open the door just as

Cherise almost falls out of Trina's Mercedes, a bag held tightly in her hands.

"Hey guys!" I yell, anticipation of the night's festivities making me louder than normal.

"Hey!" They chorus back.

Moving in unison—if you call three women bumping into each other like drunk monkeys unison—they fall into the house, dropping sweaters and purses by the door to be retrieved later. After placing overnight bags in the bedrooms they would be using, I returned to the living room. All of them were digging into the food tray and I quickly joined in. Fingers and laughter fly as we rib each other about something or another.

Trina finishes her snack first, as usual. While still licking her fingers she asks, "So, what are we gonna be reading, Zay?" My friends all call me Zay. My business associates stick to Zariah.

I smile, knowing I had a "hot property" to introduce. One thing about women...if it's juicy, they're game. "It's a new manuscript I got from a waitress up at the Coffee Hut. I saw a sign about an author reading and when I inquired, she mentioned she was a budding author herself. I told her about our book club and offered to discuss it and give her feedback."

"Shit! You couldn't find nothing from somebody we already know? I don't want to read no jacked-up story by some chick on the street. I wanna know what to expect!" Trina grimaces as she pours a finger of some dark whiskey into a tumbler. "A waitress. What's her name anyway? Chiquita?"

"Don't be so narrow-minded. Every author is a chick or brother on the street until somebody starts buying their books. And no, her name's not Chiquita. It's Sydney Molare'," I tell her Trina-short-for-Quantrinique fronting, uppity ass. I mean, we're cool and all, but sometimes Trina puts on airs and it grates on my last nerve when she does.

"Yeah. You got to start somewhere. Besides, you always complain unless it Eric Jerome Dickey or Zane or somebody hot. It's time we got some new blood in here. I say let's read it." Cherise pipes up and crosses her arms, eyes focused hard on Trina.

"Me too," Travesteen chimes in.

"If this shit is jacked up, I'm leaving after the first chapter and you can take Ms. Steen and the gay Lady Godiva home," Trina pouts. "Sydney Molare'. Sounds like a French drag queen or something."

"Does not. She's black, just like your skillet-bottom butt. I've started reading it and I ga-ran-*tee* you won't be going anywhere once we get into it. Besides, if you keep drinking that whiskey, you aren't going anywhere anyway." I tell her pointedly as she adds more liquor to her glass. One thing about Trina, she's always BYOB.

"Yeah. Yeah. Don't worry about me. I know how to hold my Jack. What's this book supposed to be about?"

"A relationship," I smirk.

"Every book is about a relationship," Trina whines. "What's she gonna tell us we haven't already heard about over and over again and—"

"What does it matter?" Cherise cuts in. "Damn! Let's give this chick the benefit of the doubt. If it becomes a best seller, your bourgeois ass can say you were one of the first reviewers of it."

"I just *love* relationship stories. They help me know how to handle this situation or that one," Travesteen sighs.

They're probably the reason you've had four husbands, too.

"Trina, shut up and let's get on with it," Travesteen growls. Turning to me, she asks, "What's it called?"

"*Small Packages.*"

"Uhmmmm. That's a book I would *definitely* buy if I passed it in the store. The title alone draws me into it." Travesteen nods her head like a bobbing duck.

Ditsyness is no recognizer of person.

"Sounds like a small-dick-but-good-lover-nevertheless type of story to me. And you know that shit ain't *even* true. Not in *my* book, anyway," Trina spits out.

"Yeah, yeah, we all know how you like your men—rough, no neck, and with plenty of muscles below the waist." Cherise paints a crude picture with her fingers.

"That's right! I need somebody who doesn't mind getting rough and dirty between the sheets! I know you wouldn't know nothing about that though, would you, Cherise?" Trina laughs at this last statement.

"Now, don't you start, Trina," I inject. The last thing I needed was for a squabble to cloud a good story. "Let me get the manuscript and we'll get started." I walk into my sanctuary/bedroom and retrieve the manuscript from the mantle. Reentering the living room, I say, "Everybody get comfortable 'cause this is gonna be a wild read."

Trina snorts but doesn't say anything. Cherise and Travesteen look at the manuscript eagerly, but I wait, letting the tension build.

"Girl, what you waiting on? Let's get our *read* on!" Travesteen finally yells.

"Yeah. Let's read!" Cherise echos.

"Okay, okay. Here we go…"

SMALL PACKAGES
CHAPTER 1

Whew!

I trudge up the stairs to my apartment feeling beat. My feet are like two barking dogs—yapping with each stair I ascend. The moist heat of the air lies on my back like a heavy hand, curling my hair along my forehead and neck. I wipe the sweat from my brow and grasp the railing to aid me up the next stairwell, hoping to reach the cool comfort of my apartment quickly.

I'm not really commiserating though, just a little down. Today's my birthday and I have no one to celebrate it with and no where to go. A whole weekend with no prospects to put a moment of sunshine in my life. Labor Day weekend at that. Great. Add another day of sitting around lonely.

I sigh thinking about all the time on my hands and trying to forget the numerous things I didn't finish at Tylos, the fashion house where I work. I'm a fashion designer by trade and not just a wannabe designer either. I'm a designer *extrodinaire*, if I have to say so myself. I took this job two thousand miles away from home because it was a once-in-a-lifetime deal (there aren't too many fashion centers in Mississippi).

I started sewing clothes when I was ten. There were five of us kids—three girls and two boys—tight as ticks on a dog. The boys were boys and the girls tried to be boys. We wore out every thing we got our bodies in. Like other mothers in the rural area where we lived, my mother sewed and resewed a lot of our clothes to stretch what money we had. I sat at her feet, watching her constantly. In my mind, I improved on her patterns and added my own touches; my fingers just aching to make my mental designs a reality. So, after badgering my mother (and barely avoiding a butt whipping), she finally showed me the basic stitches then I was off! I haven't looked back since.

At first, I was making the clothes everybody was wearing, but by the time I was a teenager, I started feeling stifled, repressed. I changed up the patterns and pretty soon, I was making clothes which made me feel alive. Bright, bold colors. Irregular shapes and lengths. I was a *unique!* Unfortunately, everybody else thought I was just, plain strange. They couldn't see the beauty in my designs. Pretty soon my Moma was asking me why I was making all this *mess* folks around here didn't want to wear, wasting good material and all. If I acted right, I could make plenty of money sewing all the time. Yeah right.

I started right then looking for somewhere else to go. Some place where I could be appreciated, not ridiculed. By a stroke of luck, I found a fashion school over in Florida that liked my designs and offered me a scholarship. Just as soon as they put the diploma in my hand, I was out of there like the devil was on my butt.

My folk didn't really want me going so far away but I was tired of how folks were treating me. I packed up one long-pass-decent suitcase and hopped on a bus to sunny Tallahassee.

Florida…what a whole new ball of wax. The sunshine, the crazy folks, anything goes…I was home! I took all the classes and made piece after piece. By the time I was a senior, I *knew* I was in my element. By a stroke of luck, my senior design show won first prize and a fashion designer, who just happened to be in the audience, saw my work and offered me this job out here in California. I hopped at the chance. Shoot, I definitely didn't want to go back home.

My folks felt I had been away long enough, though. They thought I could have a good living in Yokel, Mississippi making clothes for the folks around town. But after I slowly and carefully explained this was a once-in-a-lifetime, can't-put-off-until-another-day chance, they relented.

So, here I am. Homesick. Feeling lonely. Everything I thought I wouldn't be when I left Florida. Oh, I did meet a man when I first got here, but he turned out to be one of those men who like to put their hands on you and not in a friendly way. I kicked his butt to the curb. Quick. Now all he does is call and call. I hope I don't have to get a restraining order for his tail.

"You should take a page from this book, Cherise. If somebody fucks you over, get a restraining order. Do not, and I repeat, do *not* keep fucking with them." Trina snaps out.

Cherise just stares, refusing to bait her.

I begin again…

My mental soliloquy is broken as I notice the package propped up against the door of my apartment. Picking it up, I see it from my crazy,

14

childhood friend, Venetra. She was the only one in the world who encouraged me and was even *remotely* on my wavelength. The only one who would remember to send me something for my birthday. I probably have a lot of calls on my answering machine from my folks wishing me a happy birthday, but they don't usually send me anything. My heart grows heavy thinking about home.

I open the apartment door, all the while shaking the package trying to figure out what could be in it. It was probably a 9-inch by 4-inch package—too small for lingerie and not noisy or heavy enough to be jewelry. Besides, I knew Venetra couldn't afford anything too pricey and she wouldn't spend her money to send me cheap jewelry anyway.

What in the world could she have sent me?

I drop my purse and keys and kick the door close with my aching foot forgetting, for once, to glance out the panoramic windows which provided me with a great view of the park one block over. Normally, when I come in the door, I survey my large "great room" and a feeling of peace surrounds me—the soft chocolate leather sofa set, allowing me to sink into it, soothing my usually shot nerves; the drawing table set by the windows to catch all the best light; and my favorite, the leopard print chaise lounge I found sitting on the street. Not today, though. Today I'm focused on the present I just received.

Ripping at the outer paper, I slide my fingers under the tape, eager to see what my present is. Tearing the paper off, I turn the box over.

DELUXE PULSATING STIMULATOR.

What? My girl sent me a massager? I start laughing. Just like her to send me something I didn't need.

I open the box to get a look at this stimulator massager. My laughter dies in my throat and is replaced with silence. The massager is a red cylinder, probably eight inches long, two inches wide and the top of it is "knobby." This didn't look like the massagers I had seen before. In fact, it looks just like a...No! I *know* she didn't! I know Venetra didn't send me no *sex toy*!

A small piece of white paper falls out of the box. Looking down, I see the word INSTRUCTIONS across the top of it. I read through the instructions, my eyes growing wider and wider, as I read suggestion after suggestion.

Oh...my...goodness! It *is* a sex toy!

I race over to the phone to call Venetra. My fingers dialing by memory a number I'd dialed a thousand times before.

"Hello?" Venetra's husky voice purrs in the phone.

"You can just quit talking like that. I ain't yo' man," I tell her. She always answered the phone a "certain" way when she was expecting her flavor-of-the-month to call.

"Hey, girl! Did you get my gift?" I hear the excitement in her voice.

"Yeah! Why do you think I'm calling?"

"You tried it out yet?" Just like her tail to ask me something like this.

"No! Why did you send me this *mess*?"

"Why you think? You ain't got no man. Or did you get one since I last talked to you?" She huffs.

"No." I laugh.

"I figured. Anyway, women, you know, got needs too. Shoot, it's been months since you had some. Right?" Logical isn't she?

"A couple." So what if I don't have no man? I don't always have to have a man.

"A couple? More like doggone near a year! Look, I always say, 'If you can't get the real thing, a stand in is just as good.'"

"Did she say a whole year?" Travesteen interrupts. "I would just *die* if I didn't get me some loving in a year."

"We know. That's why you in the fix you in right now, missy." Trina laughs.

"Girls, stop interrupting! You're gonna miss something." I say, slightly annoyed.

"Yeah, yeah," Trina waves her hands for me to continue.

"Girl, you crazy!" Plumb foolish.

"I'll bet you ain't even using your finger for nothing but sewing and housework."

"Shut up!" I say, mortified she even *suggested* it.

"See, that's what I'm talking about. Your stiff behind ain't had none since Moses parted the Red Sea and you ain't trying to help yourself out. I, personally, don't see how you do it. Before I met my latest, my index finger was about to lose its nail, the way I was working it."

"You are sick!" I laugh as the image forms in my mind.

"No. I am fulfilled. Girl, try it out! I *know* you won't regret it!"

"I...don't...know," I hesitate. I'm not a freaky, put-a-dildo-in-your-coochie type of girl. I mean, what's wrong with regular sex? Okay, maybe I kick in a little oral now and then, but I've got to know you for a *while.*

"You don't know? You don't *know*? Girl, get the cobwebs out of your stuff and try out the toy! Shoot, the way you acting, you would think it was a crime. Well, it *ain't* against the law. Take a bath and turn on them damn batteries! Ugh, I got a beep. Talk to you later. Bye!"

I just stare at the phone. I'll bet her trifling ass didn't even get a beep.

Replacing the phone in its cradle, I pick up the "stimulator" again. After studying it all over, I run my fingers over the knobs at the top. I am surprised at how soft and pliable it feels. I couldn't mistake it for skin, but it was smooth and as I squeeze, squishy.

Now how the world is all this supposed to fit in me?

I just didn't see how, so I tossed it and the instructions back in the box and took it to my bedroom. I quickly strip out of my clothes and head into the bathroom for a shower. The hot water stings my tired legs and back. I let it sluice over my head and neck as my mind wandered to the last time I was intimate.

When was it? Has it really been almost a year?

Yeah, just before I left Florida. I smile as I remember my last encounter with Willie.

Wild Willie.

It's what I called him anyway 'cause he always did things over the top. Extremes. You know, he couldn't just eat a hamburger and fries, he had to have a hamburger, fries, salad and an apple pie. He couldn't just buy one shirt, he had to buy five. He couldn't stay at an inexpensive hotel, he *only* stayed at the Radisson. We couldn't make love once or twice, we had to make love until the sun came up.

You couldn't tell it by looking at him, though. He looked so "normal." Nondescript. Blended into the crowd.

Thinking about Willie, makes me tingle: The tender kisses which turned into bruised lips; making love on the kitchen counter, breaking the table under our weight; doing our thing on the first floor terrace, knowing any interested neighbor could get an eyeful at any time. Oh, Willie was something else. Shoot! I wonder what he's doing now? Probably taking somebody else on a "Willie" trip.

My stuff is aching by this time. The spray from the shower feels like needles on my sensitized flesh. I turn off the shower and towel off, trying to avoid rubbing certain areas too hard.

Oooooh!

My nub jumps as I accidentally brush it with the towel. I fan at my face. I am hot as Hades! Taking care, I finish drying off the rest of my body, avoiding the lower body, figuring my privates could "drip dry."

Striding into the bedroom, I search for my old pajamas. I thought if I took my mind off sex, sex would take its mind off me...hopefully.

As I walk towards the kitchen to make a sandwich, the fabric from my pajamas wedges between my wet legs, the material sending sparks up through my privates. I try to unwedge the pajamas and inadvertently brushed against my old sensitive nub.

Oh!

This sets up a throbbing I feel to my breasts. Think food. Think sandwich. Ring phone! Anything to get my mind off sex!

19

I open the refrigerator, but suddenly, I don't feel hungry. Slamming the door in frustration, I walk back towards the bedroom. I'll just watch some television; ignore the throbbing.

My eyes are drawn to the stimulator as I enter the room. I stop in the doorway and stare at it.

What was it Venetra said? 'Next best thing.' I don't think so.

Curious nevertheless, I walk over to the package and lift the stimulator out. Sitting on the bed, I turn the dial on the bottom to the first setting. The wand started undulating slowly up and down like a snake. I am amazed. As I turn the dial to the next setting, the undulating gets faster. I continue through the settings until I reach the highest one—the stimulator is now just vibrating in my hands. The vibrations, in concert with my throbbing, are really turning me on.

Where is a man when you really need one?

Against my will, I close my eyes and imagine Willie here. Touching the wand to my nipples, I moan from the sensations I am feeling. Oh, it feels so *good,* much better than I thought it would.

I open my pajama top and press it lengthwise across both nipples. I cry out as nerve endings pulse and throb. Falling backwards onto the bed, I let the pings and zings wash over me; imagine I am someplace else, with someone else.

Moving the wand down my stomach, I stick it into my navel. Willie was always fond of licking my navel, but Willie never made it feel like this!

I turn the settings down until the wand is undulating again. It felt like a tongue licking in and out. In and out.

My stuff is leaking. I am *so* turned on. If it feels this good in my navel, I can only imagine what it must feel like on my mound. Anticipation makes me move the wand lower and lower, through my bush and onto my—

BBBRRRRIIINNNNGGG!

What?!

I shoot up out of my bed, momentarily disoriented. The phone rings again and again and again. I pick it up with shaky hands, trying to get it before the answering machine clicks on.

"Ah…hello?" I say in an unsteady voice.

"Analisa? That you?" my mother asks.

"It's me, Moma." *Dog! Why did she have to call now?*

"You ain't never lied!" Travesteen huffs. "It's getting good, then her mama calls."

"Girl, mamas always know when their baby girls are about to get their mack on. They got coochie ESP," Trina says with amusement. "Go on, Zay."

"I was starting to worry. What took you so long to get to the phone?" I hear the concern in her voice.

"I was in the shower, that's all." That's not all, but I can't tell her the rest.

"Oh. I was just calling to wish you a Happy Birthday."

"Thanks, Moma."

"What did you do today?"

21

"Just work, work and work some more." She didn't need to know everything.

"You didn't do anything special?"

"No. I don't really know too many people out here yet."

"When you gonna get to know somebody? You been gone almost a year." Here she goes again.

"These things take time," I say placatingly.

"That Halston fella ain't still bothering you, is he?" I hear her hackles rise through the phone.

"His name was Halmont and no, he's not bothering me."

"Well, good. I don't know why you can't meet some nice men. I told you to watch out for them crazy ones, didn't I?" Moma in overdrive is hard to stop.

"Yes, Moma, you did." Over and over again.

"You ain't out there but a hot minute and you get a looney toon. All the men in California and you find the crazies."

I remain silent, knowing she is going to keep talking until she gets tired.

"So, have you found a new boyfriend or what?" Hope brightens her voice.

"Or what," I mumble as I look at the wand still vibrating on the bed.

"What did you say?"

"I said not yet. I haven't found anyone new yet."

"Well, keep looking. Did you get the present Venetra sent? I saw her the other day and she said she sent you something she thought you needed. What was it?"

I gulp. As nosy as my Moma is, I ought to tell her Venetra sent me a vibrator. But, I'm scared she might have a heart attack or worse, *not* have a heart attack and come out here. "She sent me a massager," I manage to say.

"Well, isn't that nice? I'm sorry I didn't think of it myself. You use it on your feet and back to help with your soreness. Those massagers are great."

"Yeah, they are." In ways you don't realize.

"Is it a plug in kind or does it work with batteries?"

"Batteries."

"Good. That way you can use it wherever you want—the living room, kitchen, bathroom or the bedroom. Of course, if it was electric, you would only have to plug it in, but the batteries make it more convenient."

"Yes, it does." It surely does. This way, I won't get electrocuted.

"Well, make sure you get some spares. Ain't nothing worse than coming home tired and your massager has died."

"I can imagine." Or I think I can once I get you off the phone.

"Oh, the other reason I called is your cousin Myra is getting married in two months and she wants you to make her dress."

My ears perk up. "Somebody is marrying Myra?" Myra is my cousin on my mother's side. She is 250-lbs. wet and has an attitude as big as her body. Must be some miserable man out there to settle for her.

"Yes, she is. She found her a good man, too. He works for Amtrak, has his own house, his own car and no children. I think she did good for herself."

"Sounds like it." How did big Myra find a man and I can't?

"She told me to tell you she wants something traditional, maybe an A-line skirt and some lace at the top."

"Well..."

"She also told me to tell you she didn't want nothing way-out, making her look wild or big."

I choke on a laugh. "She *is* big."

"She ain't really *big*. She just has big *bones*. I've been telling y'all that all your lives. Anyway, make her something to slim her down."

"Moma, I design clothes. I'm *not* Jenny Craig." I say with annoyance. Who am I supposed to be? The Fairy Godmother?

"What are you saying? Why, that girl hardly eats at all."

Not in front of your face, I want to say. She didn't gain weight breathing air and eating Nutribars all day.

"All right. I'll make her something to slim her down... somehow," I say, knowing all along, unless I find a bootleg prescription of Fen-phen, she will probably be *larger* than I remembered.

"Thank you, baby. I'll tell her you'll do it," she says, sounding relieved.

Great. Put the monkey on my back, will you.

"Well, you take care and get plenty of rest."

"I will Moma."

"Moma loves you."

"I love you too, Moma."

"Bye."

"Bye."

I hang up the phone and look at the vibrator snaking itself on the bed and I can't help but laugh. I sure hope my Moma doesn't visit and want to use the "massager."

24

Well, I'm *definitely* cooled off. Thanks, Mom. I put the vibrator back in the box and place it on the top shelf of the closet. Maybe another day.

"So, what do you think so far?" I ask.

Trina, of course, is the first to offer her opinion. "Chick is a prude and her friend is a freak!"

I roll my eyes heavenward.

"Just because she sent a vibrator? Don't you have a vibrator?" Cherise stares at Trina, one eyebrow lifted.

"Yeah, but I'll bet I don't have *nearly* the experience with it you do!" Trina retorts.

"You're so funny. There's nothing wrong with sex toys," Cherise insists.

"Spoken like the true lesbian you are."

"Y'all be quiet!" Travesteen yells, hands fanning the air. Turning to me, she says, "Zay, I like it. I think I like it partially because she's from Mississippi, like us, but I also like hearing about other folks...sex experiences."

"She hadn't had no 'sex experiences' yet," Trina snickers.

"She will and I can hardly wait to hear about it. I sure hope her mama doesn't keep interrupting, though. Let's go on," Travesteen nods eagerly.

"Get ready 'cause here we go...."

CHAPTER 2

The dream was so real. So vivid.

Willie is licking my lips, his legs intertwined in mine. Biting and licking at the lower lip, then the upper, his hands slowly, methodically, roaming over my stomach. My hands are shoved into his short dreads, kneading and pulling, trying to keep us melded together.

Wicked lips make a slow, thorough descent into the valley of my breasts. I shift my chest, my nipples trying to find his mouth; wanting some suckling. Lips finally locate the sensitized tips and I inhale sharply.

Oh! The sensations of his tongue; his teeth gnawing me gently.

My hands roam all over his naked torso, tangling in his thick back hair, wondering again why women didn't like hair on men. It made them so masculine to me. Sexy.

His tongue trails a steady path downward. My nipples protest at the quick treatment; yearn for the warmth of his mouth again. I tug at his dreads, beseeching him upwards, settling him back on my tingling nipples.

Thick fingers are in my bush, searching for the opening to my Eden. My fingers linger in his chest hair and move downward, trying to feel "Mr. Big."

Willie shifts his body, allowing my fingers to just miss their mark. His lips follow the path of his hands. I clench as I feel him part my nether lips and lean towards my bounty, his warm breath blowing over my mons. I shift my legs wider, making room for this sensual assault on my body. As I settle my legs over his shoulders, I arch my pelvis forward, wanting his tongue; craving the licking.

His tongue works its magic. He is the puppet master and I have plenty of stings for him to pull. His tongue darts slowly in and out. In and out. Fingers push along with his tongue, filling me up, opening me wide.

I lift sharply as his whiskers rub along the tip of my nub…pushing me towards the brink. I shift his head upwards, needing a moment to collect myself, not ready to reach my peak just yet.

I watch as he sits back on his knees, his sex jutting outwards. Wait a minute…"Mr. Big" isn't how I remember. It's red and slowly moving up and down like a…like a charmed snake!

What is going on here?

I want to pinch myself, but I want what the dream offers too much to wake up.

He takes my reluctant hand and places it on the new "Mr. Big." The tip slowly grazes my palm, vibrating as it touches. I'm mesmerized as the tip contacts me again and again. I slowly begin to anticipate the touch; want the vibrating feeling to come over and over again. Finally, I grasp it with my entire hand, the softness of it surprising me. I watch as my hand flows upwards and downwards, mimicking the movements of his wand, the vibrations sending unknown messages to my throbbing nub.

Willie gently lays me back and pushes towards my Eden. The tip touches my opening…

My eyes flip open.

"Darn it! Why does she have to wake up now?" Travesteen squeals. "She was just getting to the good part!"

"Girl, you are a mess!" Trina hoots.

"I mean, what happens next?" Travesteen persists, confusion clearly on her face.

"If you guys will hold up, we can find out." Irritation creeps into my voice.

"Yeah, let her read it. I want to hear this," Cherise whines.

"Something new for you, I'll bet. Or is it?" Trina questions.

"Shut...up." Cherise waves me on.

I stare at the white ceiling wondering where I am and momentarily wondering what has happened to Willie. As reality sets in, I realize my hands are shoved into my pajama bottoms and I'm horny as all get out.

Shoot! Why did I have to wake up before the good part?

"That's exactly what I said too." Travesteen interjects.

"We heard you the first time!" I tell her.

Travesteen just rolls her eyes.

As I begin to extricate my hands from my pajamas, I rub hard against my mound.

Ahhhh. What am I feeling?!

Of their own accord, my fingers begin to pluck and rub at my nub slowly, feeling the stiffness and softness of the contours and folds, then faster and faster as my juices flow over my fingers, making the entire area slick and slippery.

I've never felt anything even remotely like this. No man has ever touched me just... like...this.

Applying pressure where the need is great; rubbing lightly where I'm extra sensitive, my fingers continue on, directed by the invisible nubbal instructions received only by them. Delving and thrusting. Pushing and stroking. I push one, two, then three fingers inside of me. Slowly, then pumping.

Oh my goodness!

I struggle to push my pajamas and panties off, giving me more room to work. As I wrestle with the pants around my legs, my eyes rest on the vibrator in the top of my closet.

What the heck? If my fingers make me feel this good, the vibrator should really do the trick.

I hastily retrieve it from its box and turn it to the highest setting. Laying back on the bed, I thrust the vibrator onto my nub.

Yow!

It felt like thousands of volts of electricity were delivered to my sensitive flesh! I turn the settings down until it is only wiggling a bit and replace it.

Uhm, yes.

The vibrator is making my stiff button stiffer. I feel the blood rushing to the area; my sex lips engorging. Fingers trail behind, in front, and with the movement of the vibrator. I part my lips and gently shove it inside.

Oh, the rush! My womb feels like it is trying to extrude itself; place its opening directly on the vibrating tip. Hit bottom.

I gently shove and pull the vibrator in and out. In and out. Flowing with the movements.

My fingers resuming residence on my lonely nub, rubbing in a circular motion, around and around, faster and faster, until I feel an intense tingling start in my toes and move rapidly up my legs, to my sex lips and finally...explode at my nub. I ride the wave of hot hormones, not wanting it to stop. Bucking without control until the tingling slows, then finally ceases.

Ohmyohmyohmyohmyohmyoh*my*!   What was *that?*

I cup my sex, squeeze my legs around my hand, and roll onto my side—the sweat cooling on my flesh; my hair wild around my head. *I can't believe what just happened! Why can't men make it feel this good?* Finally, I sit up. Removing the vibrator, I turn it off.

Invigorated, I stand and walk to the sliding glass door leading off to the balcony and open it. I never put any curtains up since I'm so far up. Until I notice a peeping Tom, I won't.

I step naked onto the balcony. A warm breeze is blowing, making my hair fly about my face. Glancing over the balcony, my heavy breasts lying on the cool railing, I rub myself up and down.

Amazed at my boldness.

Feeling alive.

Fulfilled.

I breathe in the night air, unconcerned about any neighbors; unselfconscious in my nakedness. It's 3 o'clock in the morning and the only ones I should be worried about were across from me. All the windows are dark, so I feel safe alone in my nakedness.

Suddenly, a red glow out of the corner of my eye catches my attention. I strain my eyes trying to see if I imagined it or not. The glow returns on a balcony across and to my left, one apartment down. As I watch, the glow reappears again.

What could it be?

I continue to watch and wait, not trying to shield my nakedness. Not caring if someone saw. After all, none of these people know me.

A dark shape disengages from the shadows and leans on the railing—a large man, by the outline. I couldn't tell anything about his features, though. All I did know was he was getting an eyeful and I didn't care. In fact, I felt horny again.

I swayed against the railing, my body calling out for something; sending a pheromonic message irrespective of my conscious brain.

After a few minutes of him just standing there, he gives me a shadowy salute and I hear the terrace sliding door open, then close. I remain standing there.

Swaying and wanting.

Wondering who he was.

As my body cools down, I return to my bedroom. I lay down on sheets musty with the scent of my self-play and fall into a deep, comalike sleep.

"Zay, turn the air up 'cause I think Cherise is starting to get hot," Trina laughs. "Brings back memories, doesn't it?"

"For you too, hussy. You know you've played with a vibrator or two, so don't—" Cherise begins.

"Yeah, but I wasn't *a-lone,*" Trina mouths off. "It was always part of the foreplay, not the whole act. *Fore*...play."

"I can't speak for anybody else, but I sure wouldn't mind meeting this Willie person," Travesteen says suddenly. "Do you know if he's really real, Zay?"

"What? You want me to ask the waitress?" Sarcasm drips from my lips.

"Could you?" Travesteen asks innocently.

"Yeah, right after I beat some damn sense into your head!" I say, shaking my fist at her.

"Girl, I know a brother just like Willie. His name was Kevin, though. If you want, I can give you the digits," Trina offers.

"*Puh*-lease! The last thing Steen needs is another phone number. Get her the vibrator instead. It will save her plenty of dough," Cherise huffs.

"Listen to the girl. She's got *experience* in these matters," Trina replies with a knowing nod at Cherise.

"Keep on messing with me," Cherise volleys.

"I intend to."

"Any of y'all ever walked around naked in a public place?" Travesteen asks dreamily.

"Are you crazy? Of course we haven't!" Trina yells, lips pursed. "I ain't interested in sharing everything I got with folks I don't even know. Besides, there's 'Peeping Toms' everywhere. You see what just happened to her."

"I'm just saying, don't you think it would be so...*erotic*...to walk around flashing your goodies for the world to see and they don't know you, can't get to know you? It sounds so *delicious,*" Travesteen sighs.

"I think so, too. I've never done it but I've... *thought* about it." Cherise stares at the floor.

Me too.

"Y'all just straight-up freaky, exhibitionist heffas! What if somebody came and saw you walking around butt-naked or knocking boots in public? You just *might* get too much action! You will sho' nuff be freaked out if somebody gets you in a dick sandwich!" Trina exclaims, hands on her ample hips.

"Trina, now what man is gonna let another man get his groove on with his woman while he's there?" I ask her loud behind. "He's not going to want to share what he's got with some man just showing up out of nowhere."

"Yeah. I mean, if you got to wonder about him like that, why deal with him in the first place? You got to be scrapping the bottom of the barrel if he's all you can get. You hard up or something, Trina?" Cherise smirks.

"I ain't never been hard up for shit! I can get a man…and a woman too, if I wanted one." Her eyes snap at Cherise.

"Naw. Ain't no woman wanting to put up with your ass. You've got a bad attitude," Cherise replies matter-of-factly. Travesteen and I both laugh.

"And I'm gonna get a worser one if some big booty, soft leg steps to me trying to bump my monkey!"

"Why don't we just get back to the story?" I say and begin reading before somebody came to blows.

•

Willie was back. I felt his hands crawling up my thighs and brushing through my mound hair. His lips were fastened on my neck. Sucking.

My hands reach around and palm his hairy buttocks as he pushes his sex into the soft flesh of my hips. I feel the arousal, then the slow movements and vibrations—the new "Mr. Big" was still with him.

I turn over to face him. He parts his lips and sticks his tongue deep down my throat, twisting and playing, faster and faster, until I almost bite his in response.

Removing his lips from mine, he fastens them on my chest, suckling and nibbling. He rains light kisses on my breasts before moving straight to the navel. I feel his tongue probing and licking; sucking at the flesh of my stomach. I cup my breasts and pinch the hard buttons.

My juices are beginning to leak. I feel it slowly crawl down my opening and between my cheeks.

Willie's fingers splay me open and with a stiff tongue, he begins to lap at the juices. I clench my fists in his hair, moving his face up and down where I need him; pushing my mound into his mouth, trying to make his tongue fill me up completely. My fingers enter into the play, rubbing and mashing at my nub.

I'm headed towards Nirvana.

Willie quickly replaces his mouth with his magic wand. As I open wider, the snaking wand moves towards me. He presses his tip to my nub, letting the vibrations move through me; tripping my heartbeat. I can hardly breathe.

He slowly pushes the tip inside. The undulations force my opening wider and wider, my juices lubricating his path. As he pushes in completely, my body shudders. The combined sensations—vibration and undulation—inside me is so intense. Vaginal muscles spasming uncontrollably, squeezing and releasing. As he begins stroking, I move with him, trying not to lose the contact; needing to feel every tidbit of his skin inside of me.

The pressure builds and I move faster, gyrating to my own rhythm. Willie keeps up with me and it's a wonder the sheets don't catch on fire from the friction. Just like before, I feel the tingling begin in my feet and move up my legs. I can't help but whimper as the tingling reaches my nub and the light explodes behind my closed lids...

I open my eyes.

"Ah!" I say sharply as I see Travesteen opening her mouth to speak. Thankfully, she snaps it close.

The early light of morning is spilling through the sliding doors. Willie is gone, but I can still *feel* him. Moving my hands downwards, I realize the massager is between my legs. Its humming, vibrating and undulating is beginning to irritate my sore tissues. I remove it and turn it off, placing it on the nightstand.

As I raise off the bed, I notice a man sitting on his terrace...watching me. It appears to be the same balcony *and* the same man from last night.

The man is big and dark as midnight. I couldn't see his features from here, but I could tell he was built like Adonis. A cigarette was held in one hand and a glass in the other. As I meet his eyes, he smiles and salutes.

It *is* the man from last night! The glow I saw must have been his cigarette.

I hurriedly wrap myself in the bedsheet, the light of day making me feel self-conscious and ashamed.

I wonder how much he saw?

From his reaction, I guessed everything. I stumble towards the dresser, pull out underwear, shorts and a T-shirt, and rush into the bathroom. I stare in the mirror.

What have you done, girl?

"Shut up," I tell myself. I don't know the man and the likelihood of him figuring out who I am is slim to none. This is a security complex and nobody can get in unless they live here or somebody knows them.

Relax. He's probably safe.

As I turn on the shower, I resolve to buy those curtains after all.

"See what I mean? What if old Peepers just happens to be lying in wait someday?" Trina exclaims. "What's Miss walk-around-naked-screwing-herself-with-the-windows-open gonna do then?"

"What is it with you?" I ask irritably. Being anal retentive was not Trina's style. "It's just a story. Besides, she's acting out some stuff millions of us just think about."

"Yeah. Now that I've heard it, I *surely* want to try it out," Travesteen oozes.

"I still say that's some freaky shit. I can't ever remember wanting to rub on my clit without having a man around to see it. What's the point?" Trina clearly looks puzzled.

"A man did see it and you're *still* mad about it," I indicate.

"She didn't *invite* him to see it. He was a voyeur, not a partner." Trina explains like I'm a schoolgirl. "There is a difference."

"I still think it sounds delicious. I mean, a man you don't know, looking at you…ooohhhh!" Travesteen moans and falls back onto the couch

"*You* probably think he's husband material," Trina snorts.

"Well, Trina, since you say I'm an 'expert' at finger play, I'm gonna give you my take on what just happened," Cherise begins. "You know folks always say, 'can't nobody love a woman like a woman.' I, personally, think it's true. *But,* I also know when I'm not in a relationship, I can satisfy my own urges and needs. I don't have to just *wait* for somebody to give me some relief. I believe can't nobody love a woman like her own self can."

"You're crazy as hell." Trina frowns.

"Hmmm. That's deep, Cherise." Travesteen says, sitting up. "I'm not gonna say I don't play with my…*stuff*, but whenever I do it alone, I feel…ashamed. Like it's wrong or something." She lowers her eyes. "But, having somebody watch you…*oh Lawd*, what would my mama say if she heard me?" She clasps her hands over her mouth.

Please don't let her Gone-with-the-wind ass swoon!

"I don't think it's wrong, I just don't want it to be *all* the action I'm getting," I smile and say. "I want to have the whole shebang-a-bang-bang, if you know what I mean."

"You can. I'm just saying in the meantime and between times, you might like to see what you can do for yourself," Cherise states.

"I still say masturbating is part of foreplay and that's all. I know men like to see us playing with ourselves…but doing it just for myself? No way. And not for no freeloaders looking, either." Trina slugs her drink back.

"Admit it, Trina. Your ass is just a sexually repressed, not-satisfied-in-the-least, undercover, ghetto 'ho trying to keep the closet door closed with some raggedy assed Scotch tape." Cherise slings the words at Trina and they hit their mark.

"Who you calling a ghetto 'ho? Girl—" Trina snarls.

"If the damn bra fits—" Cherise spits back.

"Ladies! Let's just cool this discussion for now!" I say hurriedly. *Things are getting hot up in here!*

"Naw, she wanna call somebody a ghetto 'ho! I'll tell her who the 'ho is!"

"Trina! Let's keep it clean!" I yell, knowing where she was going with her statement. Playing the dozens would get somebody's ass whipped and we're too old to be fighting like schoolgirls. Breathing heavily, they stare at each other but don't say anything else to ignite the gasoline-doused charcoals. "Now, it sounds like this book is really opening up some great discussions, but I'm not gonna read another page if you can't control yourselves."

"Y'all try to get along. I wanna hear the rest of her story," Travesteen begs.

"You think you two can do that?" I inquire. "I'm starting to dig it, but I can just put it up and read it all by myself." I close the manuscript and start to rise, intent on proving my point.

"NO!" They yell in unison.

"Zay, girl, you know me and Cherise always gonna be johning one another. We cool, though." Trina says with forced brightness.

"Yeah." Cherise agrees with the same level of forced cheerfulness. "I ain't mad at her. Besides, she can't help it."

"Oh, good. They've made up. Let's read on, Zay." Travesteen claps her hands happily.

I stare at them, gauging their heat-o-meter readings. When I'm satisfied they aren't about to come to blows, I begin again.

CHAPTER 3

The twenty-minute drive to the shopping center takes nearly an hour due to an accident—a huge pile up involving a 18-wheeler and four cars. The ambulances and police cars choke the highway and cars cram along the sides looking for an opening so they could reach the next exit.

After thirty minutes of sitting in the heat with the motor off and the windows down, I am sticky from the moisture. I'm *definitely* reconsidering those curtains. I look around, hopelessly, for an opening in traffic. Any small space which would allow me to turn my Galant around.

Finally, I see the wrecker pull the last car and one lane opens. The police slowly reroute traffic around the broken glass and lone fender lying in the road. All the "smart" roadside drivers try to wedge into traffic; the tired, law-abiding citizens reluctant to let them in, almost causing another mishap. As I watch the snails speeding past the car, my lane begins to move and I head for the mall.

The shopping center is crowded even at this early hour. I ride around the same lanes three times before I spot a car pulling out. I wait patiently, irritating the held up drivers behind me, before parking into the vacated spot. The car waiting behind me blasts me with a long blow of his horn. Oh well. Everybody in the city knows how it works. Don't come to a crowded mall if you're in a hurry. I lock the car door and quickly walk through the melting heat into the cool air of the mall.

As I meander through the mall, I check out every clothing store I pass and mentally comment on the routine, identical fare each offers. You would think people would get tired of looking alike. Not for this girl. Today, I'm wearing a pair of low-slung jeans which cling, but don't hug so tight you can see my panty-line, my favorite cherry halter and a fringed scarf wrapped around my hips. A bandanna is tied around my lower locks and hangs down my back. A belly chain sets off my outfit. As I notice the admiring glances, I know my "style" is on time.

I locate the Bed &Bath at the far end of the mall. The place is mobbed due to a 50% off sale. I rummage around in the bins, quickly dismissing the huge cabbage prints and busy color ensembles which make my head hurt, until I finally settle on some white sheers. Not my usual, but it's what I think I need to calm some of my fears, but not make me a prisoner in my own apartment.

Just as I exit the store, I hear someone calling my name.

"Analisa! Analisa!"

I turn towards the voice and to my horror it's Halmont—the last man on earth I ever wanted to see again.

Halmont is a tall, high-yellow brother with "good" hair and model looks. At one time, I thought he was my knight in shining armor. Instead he turned into a roadkill armadillo—rotten and stinking. He is dressed in a T-shirt, khaki shorts and dress socks with sandals. City-country at its best.

I refuse to turn away since I know it would just be a waste of time. I've seen him and he knows I've seen him. I wait, dreading the meeting but reluctant to create a scene I know he doesn't mind participating in.

"Analisa! Girl, you looking *good!*" He grabs me and pulls me into a hug while I stiffen my body. I can barely stand to have this toad looking at me, much less touching me.

"Hello, Halmont."

"Girl, it's been so long. Too long. What's been going on?" He asks eagerly.

"Nothing. Work, work, and more work." I'm trying to *act* friendly at least.

"Still working hard I see. All work and no play makes Analisa a dull girl." He smiles and the even rows of white teeth look obscene on such a waste of a man.

"I play."

"I've been calling and calling and I can't seem to get anything but the answering machine." He looks at me with a question in his eyes.

"I must be out if that's all you are getting." Answer your own damn question. You know the deal.

"I miss you, girl. I'm really sorry about the misunderstanding we had and all. I don't know why you reacted like that."

"You don't, huh?" Is this morose idiot trying to make me believe him?

"I mean, all the girls I ever dated never once freaked out when I gave them a little swat." He is bobbing his head like he's really saying something good.

41

"I don't think a slap in the face is a swat," I point out.

His face contorts, "It wasn't no *real* slap. I just tapped you lightly."

"Like I told you then, don't *nobody* hit me in the face. *Joke* or not."

"Ok, ok." He holds his hands up in front of him. "I don't want to get hung up on some past history."

"Past is a relative term." I'm not giving this woman-handling buffoon one inch.

"Look, I know yesterday was your birthday and all. I didn't remember it until I saw you and I said to myself, 'Self, you ought to take Analisa out for dinner to celebrate her birthday.'"

"You said all that, did you?"

"Yes, I did." He smiles, pleased with himself.

I shift my bags to the other hand and say, "Halmont, it's been great seeing you again, but I have to pass on the dinner."

As I begin to walk around him, he stops me with a finger to the center of my chest. I feel his hand fold and the knuckles graze my breast.

I know he didn't do that!

I swat the offending hand off my chest and stand there breathing heavily, trying not to say something which would make the sudden tension in the air explode.

"Don't...*ever*...touch...me...again," I say through clenched teeth.

His eyes become half-lidded, suggestive. At one time I thought I could drown in those eyes, now I want to stab one out with my keys.

"You know you want me. All women do. I'm every woman's fantasy, including yours."

"A legend in *your* own mind."

"Girl, why you so hard? Bitter women get unattractive fast."

"Well, consider me bitter and scratch me off your list of available victims."

I turn quickly and walk off, but not before I see a weird look cross his face. I increase my pace, expecting him to grab my arms at any moment. Ducking into a furniture store, I watch the area behind me in a huge antique mirror. I didn't see him following me and to be honest, I probably would have torn up the store trying to get away from him. After a few more minutes of pretending I was browsing, I walk to the edge of the storefront, look in both directions and head straight for the mall exit.

I power-walk around women with strollers and through couples holding hands. I ignore the gasps and ugly stares boring holes in my back caused by my social rudeness. *Hey, I'm sorry, but after running into Halmont, if one of us is going to be mad today, it's gonna to be you.*

Reaching the exit without encountering Halmont again, I look both ways and quickly sprint across the street and to my car. Fumbling with the keys, I almost wet my pants from the anxiety pervading my body. When I finally get the door open, I collapse on the seat, my head on the steering wheel. Safe. Thank goodness, I'm safe.

A tapping on the window almost makes me scream. I quickly look at the window and a young woman is staring at me with concern on her face. I wind the window down a few inches.

"Yes?" I ask her.

"Are you all right?"

Can everyone see something is wrong?

"Yes, I'm fine."

"OK." She didn't look convinced. "You left your keys in your door and I think this is your shopping bag here on the ground." She lifts up the bag recently vacated by my nervous hands.

"Oh, thanks." I open the door and retrieve the bag and my keys. The woman looks at me once more then walks down the aisle of cars to her own.

Thank God for Good Samaritans.

I slam my door and lock it.

I've got to calm down. It's been months since I'd seen Halmont and he shouldn't still be getting to me like this.

Images flash into my head of the last unpleasant date we had. Me realizing that underneath the handsome façade lay a man with some very "caveman" ideas about women and didn't mind telling and expressing them. I shudder at the memory; my anxiety level rising again.

I hurriedly crank my car, back out of the space and zip down the row towards the shopping center exit. I barely miss clipping a car driving diagonally across the empty spaces, ignoring the driving lanes. A blast of my horn earns me a quick flip of the bird from the teenager steering the car.

I stop the car and wonder about what I was going to do next. I didn't want to go home in case Halmont showed up and I didn't know anybody I could hang out with so, I resumed driving, taking the exit leading away from my apartment. When I see the beach sign, I suddenly decide a change of scenery would be good for me.

■

The beach is crowded with families, teenagers and couples. Some of those older couples sure could have taken advantage of the new "mature" line of swimwear I'd just finished designing. The bunches of cellulite and huge stomachs could use some slimming down.

Finding a parking space quickly, I hop out of the car. I wasn't dressed for the beach, but so what? The sun fries neurons as I walk down the boardwalk. Buying a snowcream from the first stand I reach, I eagerly push it between my lips. The mixture of flavored ice and ice cream soothes my frayed nerves.

I claim a seat on the plaza beneath a short palm tree and people watch. The sea gulls rise and dip as kids throw bread, chips and other food off the waterfront dock. Everybody seems relaxed and happy.

After two hours of this, I feel a little calmer, but to be truthful, the day's humidity and temperature were cramping the solitude. I walk back to the car determined not to be afraid in my own apartment. Shoot, if Halmont shows up, I'll just call the police. I will *not* be intimidated.

"She should have pimp-slapped his ass!" Trina, of course, yells.

"No...she did right." Travesteen straightens her shoulders and looks not at me, but behind me. "She was a real lady...and a real lady does not make a... public spectacle of herself," she says slowly. So slowly, I wonder if she'd had a similar experience.

"But he had the nerve to step to her after he had *hit* her and to top it all off, he copped a feel!" Trina says, still yelling.

"Yeah, but who's to say he wouldn't hit her again? Even in public?" Cherise asks calmly. "The police aren't private body guards. They just come when you call…sometimes."

We all sit uneasily, digesting this statement.

"I'm just saying, with jokers like him, you've got to make a stand or he's gonna constantly be pushing up on you; invading your personal space," Trina matter-of-factly states.

"You may be correct, but I'm not sure what I would do," I finally say. "My first instinct is to get as far away as possible, like she did. Is it the right reaction? I don't know."

"And you never will know until it's really you and your situation," Cherise muses.

"Let's just get back to the story." Travesteen says quietly.

●

Arriving back at my apartment complex, the apprehension returns. I survey the area before leaving the car. Not seeing Halmont lurking anywhere, I jog up the stairs and into my building, slamming the door quickly behind me and locking it.

Suddenly famished, I raid the refrigerator. A tunafish sandwich and some macaroni salad eases my hunger tremendously.

As I walk into the bedroom to hang my new sheers, I notice the balcony across the way— where my new admirer was sitting—is empty. Good. I don't think I could put up the sheers with him watching my every move. Just as I place the last clamp in the wall, I hear knocking on my door.

Wonder who that could be?

I don't have any close friends and nobody from work even knows where I live.

"Who is it?" I ask. I look through the peephole, but flowers obscure the face of the person.

"Delivery for Analisa Mathers," a deep voice says.

Great! Somebody is still thinking about me. I guessed my mother must have sent them after our chat last night. I swing the door open quickly and to my surprise, the flowers are lowered and…Halmont's face is grinning at me. I step back and try to slam the door close. Halmont stops it with his foot and roughly pushes it open wider, forcing me to stumble backwards.

"What are you doing here!" I shout.

"Girl, I told you I'm the man of your dreams and I intend to prove it," he says, a sneer on his lips.

"How the hell did you get in here?"

"What? Did you think you could keep me away? Security remembers my face from all the times I came over here when we dated and afterwards," he says with a self-satisfied smile.

I'm going to speak to the manager about the security situation just as soon as I get him out of here.

"Halmont, I think it's best you leave," I calmly state.

"I think it's best I don't," he counters.

"I'm going to call the police!" I yell, realizing the danger I was now in.

Before I take two steps towards the phone, he is on me—arms wrapped around my waist, his lips on my ears.

"Stop it, girl, you know you want me. This hard-to-get routine is getting old," he says, turning my face and pressing his lips on mine, his hands roaming freely over my chest. We tussle for a minute or so until I stomp his foot, which causes him to release me.

I run to the bedroom and close the door, but he forces it open before I turn the lock. Halmont runs towards me and tackles me onto the bed.

"Get off me!" I scream.

He presses his soggy lips to mine and I manage to bite the lower one. As he yelps and lifts off me, I roll onto the floor and scramble towards the door. Halmont cuts me off before I reach it, an angry red flush spreading across his face.

"Oh, you one of those girls that likes to play rough, I see," he says, fumbling with his belt buckle.

"No, you don't see. Just leave me alone," I say, eyes wild, looking for a way to get around him.

"I misjudged you girl. All the time I thought you were Miss Prissy and in reality you are a real tiger." Halmont lunges towards me. I manage to duck his lunge and run towards the apartment door.

"See what I mean!" Trina jumps up—spilling her drink—and points her fingers at all of us. "If she would have pimp-slapped his sorry ass in the mall, then he wouldn't be trying to rape her now!"

"Or, he might be trying to kill her now." Cherise grabs a cucumber and begins crunching loudly.

"He is definitely not a good man." Travesteen shakes her head. "Why can't they understand no means no?"

"'Cause he don't want to hear that!" Trina yells over her shoulder as she mops at her spilt drink. "I tell you, if that had of been me, one of you would be down at the courthouse posting my bail right now!"

"Trina, I don't know very many women who can whip a man. She handled it the way she thought was best. Halmont...I just wished she had better judgment in her partners," I say dejectedly.

"Don't we all?" Cherise asks around the cucumber in her mouth.

"Yeah. But like my mama always says, you have to try to make the most of any relationship. There's good and bad in everybody. Ain't nobody no saint all the time." Travesteen gives us a knowing look. "Sometimes, you win good stuff; other times, it's the booby prize."

"Well, he's definitely the booby prize here." Cherise laughs.

"I'll bet her luck will change. Let's see how she gets out of this mess." Before anything else can be said, I turn the page of the book.

I swing the door open...and run into a man standing there with his hand raised to knock. His large body envelops me in a hug, breaking my impact.

Halmont runs up the hallway and pulls up short when he sees me in this man's arms. Nobody says anything for a few seconds.

"Hey, baby. What's going on here?" The heavy, sexy voice of the stranger says in my ear.

I look up into this stranger's face and realize he seems vaguely... *familiar?* Suddenly I know. Oh my goodness, it's the man from this morning!

Is he in this with Halmont?

With this frantic thought, I try to push away from his body; looking for an escape. He holds me tight, though.

"Baby, what's wrong?" He asks again, giving me a barely perceptible shake of his head, a smile still plastered on his lips. I realize then I'm supposed to play along.

"Uhm, Halmont stopped over with some flowers and he was just leaving. Isn't that *right*, Halmont?" I manage to recover and say.

The stranger lifts his eyes from mine and looks at Halmont, who is the color of cooked lobster.

Halmont narrows his eyes and straightens his spine. "Analisa, who is this man?"

"This is my friend," I say.

"Friend? I've been watching you for a while and I don't ever recall seeing you with him. Why is that?" Halmont asks snidely.

"That is none of your business." The nerve of this jerk.

Halmont looks at the man again, bristling like he was about to make a move. A fool to the end. The stranger gently places me to the side and takes a step towards Halmont.

"I think it's about time you leave." His voice resounds with authority.

Halmont stares at the stranger, the foolish thoughts in his head showing on his face. He must have reconsidered acting on his impulses because he scowls at the man, pulls himself taller, then walks towards the door. Scooping up the bouquet of flowers he brought with him, he gives me a mean stare and walks out the door.

"Girl, you ain't even worth the trouble," he says nastily as he reaches the safety of the corridor.

"I can *fix* your smart mouth for you," the stranger says with meaning.

Halmont looks over his shoulder once more, shakes his head and goes down the stairs. The stranger walks to the stairwell and watches until Halmont gets into his car and leaves the parking lot. Then, he walks back over to me.

"You okay?" He asks with concern in his voice.

"Thank you so much. If you hadn't come along, I don't know what would have happened." I slump against the wall.

"It's all right. Who is that the guy, anyway? Boyfriend?" The stranger is watching me closely.

"Ex-friend. I considered him for a boyfriend once, but I realized early on he wasn't for me. Since then, he's been calling and sniffing around here."

The stranger nods.

I take a better look at this unknown man. He is tall, probably six-four, very dark, and heavily built. Not bodybuilder built with sculpted muscles, but "roughneck" built, with a large upper body and a flat, slim waist. He is dressed in a jersey and shorts, his feet in some Nikes. Hair is visible at the jersey's neckline and his legs are coated in it. He has an Isaac Hayes thing going on with the bald head and goatee, but Isaac Hayes doesn't have *anything* on this brother here.

He drops his keys and when he leans over to retrieve them, I get a fine view of muscles rippling in his backside. A smile forms on my lips looking at him; I feel a tingling in my stuff.

Must be all the self-exploration I've been doing lately.

I raise my eyes from his legs and hips and meet the wide smile on his lips. The air begins to crackle as I stand there staring at this gorgeous hunk of manhood that came to my rescue. Looking at him, I feel like I already know this man; like we've known each other for eons, not just a few seconds. I can't seem to drag my eyes from his face—the succulent lips, the blinding white teeth surrounded by a manicured goatee. My breath is coming faster and I just want to touch him. Hold him close.

He clears his throat and suddenly, I remember my manners. Here I am staring up in some man's face like an idiot woman.

"Would you like to come in for a soda?" I ask, feeling foolish but bold, too.

His smile gets wider. "Sure thing."

I usher him into my living room and grab a can of soda out of the refrigerator. I watch him survey the room and sit on the couch.

Uh hum. The rear view is just as good as the front view.

I hand him the cola and sit on the loveseat. "So, what brings you over to my neck of the woods?" I ask. I had never seen this man before early this morning and by coincidence he is knocking on my door.

"Well, I was in the neighborhood."

"In the neighborhood...and you just *happened* to be knocking on my door just as I opened it?"

"Sounds crazy, doesn't it?" He holds his hands up in the air, his elbows resting on the back of the couch.

"Totally *unbelievable,*" I begin laughing.

"Well, what really happened was, I was sitting on my balcony minding my own business, when I see *my woman* wrestling with some guy."

"*Your woman?*" I ask, flustered at what he said. Deep down though, him calling me his woman set my nub to thumping. I couldn't let him know that.

"Yes, *my woman*. You were out on your balcony this morning showing me everything you've got, your body whispering an ancient language to mine."

"I see."

"So, my thinking is you are *my woman* or you want to be."

"Sure of yourself, aren't you?" *Oooh. I think I want this man here.*

"Girl, I couldn't believe what I was seeing a few minutes ago. At first, I thought you were playacting or something, but since you didn't look like you were having fun, I hightailed it over here to see if I could help you out." He looks at me serious.

I am speechless. My knight has arrived. I fairly melted in my seat. Nobody has ever done anything so selfless for me before.

"I…don't know…I mean nobody… has ever done…*anything* like this for me before. I don't know how to thank you." I stammer, tears beginning to form in my eyes.

"Hey now. It's all right." He stands, walks over to the loveseat and slowly embraces me. "Shhhhh," he coos.

"You don't even know me and you come over to help me." The tears roll down my face and wet his jersey.

"I can't have men pawing over my woman and all, now can I? What kind of man would I be?"

He rocks me slowly as I continue to cry, feeling safe in his arms. When I feel composed enough to speak again, I say, "Thank you from the bottom of my heart." His inky eyes and quiet smile pull at me.

Once again, my long, lost manners rear and thrust themselves to the forefront of my mind.

Here I am wrapped up in a stranger's arms and I didn't even ask him his name. How's that for gratitude? I scoot back on the loveseat and move over to make room for him to sit down. As he sits close to me, our knees in contact with each other, the tingling I felt earlier intensifies.

"I'm Analisa Mathers. And you are?"

"Chauncey Sims, but my friends call me Chance."

"Chance. I don't think I've ever met a brother named Chance."

"Yeah, it's kind of unusual. But compared to Chauncey, I'd rather people called me Chance."

"Thank you Chance, then."

"You are welcome." He smiles again. "Hey, what did the guy bring you flowers for?"

"Yesterday was my birthday and he was one of the ones who remembered."

"Late Happy Birthday, girl. What did you get?"

"Well...I," I hesitate. *Should I tell him?*

Girl, last night you were showing him your goods, naked as the day you were born. He thinks you are "his woman" and since you kinda are considering it, tell him! My mind chides me.

"I got a little massager," I finally say.

"A massager. They're great for sore muscles aren't they?"

"Ah...yeah they are." I say a little too brightly.

Chance rubs the back of his neck then looks at me. "In fact, if it's no problem, could I borrow your massager for a minute? My neck is stiff as a board."

What do I do now? This man practically saves my life and all he asks is to use my massager which is in reality, a vibrator. How do I refuse him without looking totally stupid?

"Chance…ah, the massager is broken." I cross my fingers as I tell the lie.

"You just got it yesterday and it's broken already? Bring it out here. I'm pretty handy with things. Maybe I could fix it for you."

Well, that's that. Now, I've got to either tell him the truth or make up another unbelievable story and make him think I want him to leave. I don't want him to leave, though. I don't know this man at all, but I want to. I decide to be honest.

"Chance, the massager is not broken, but I don't think you want to use it."

"What's wrong with it?"

I hesitate. *Tell him!* "It a vibrator," I blurt out. There I said it.

"A vibrator."

"A vibrator."

"The same vibrator you were using this morning while I sipped my morning orange juice?" He looks at me with a knowing smile on his lips.

"Oh, so you *did* see me."

"Girl, after I saw you in the wee hours standing naked on the balcony, I could hardly sleep. I was up early hoping you did the buff thing all the time. Then, just as I get settled in my chair, I see you writhing all over your bed, having a good time all by yourself. I started to come over here then and help you out, but with it being early morning and all—" He leaves the sentence unfinished, but his meaning is clear.

The room is warm. I feel flush and begin fanning my face. "How much did you see?"

"See? I don't know...just you pushing that vibrator in and out and you bucking on the bed."

I gulp. He saw plenty. "I don't want you to get the wrong impression about me. I've never done anything like that before. I *definitely* don't buy sex toys."

"Hey, I'm not judging you or anything. If you like your vibrator, use it. More power to you!" He starts laughing. "You do like it, don't you?"

I start laughing now. "Yes, I do. I've never felt *anything* like it before."

"Never?"

"Never."

"Girl, you've been hanging with the wrong men."

"Yeah, that's what my Moma says, too," I begin laughing again and Chance joins in.

"So, do you go around naked on your balcony every night?"

"No! What happened was, I'd just tried out the vibrator and it made me feel so alive! So out-of-control. So free."

"The right man can make you feel like that too." His eyes become hooded.

"Maybe. Maybe not. It's going to take a really special man to outdo Redman, though."

"Who?" Chance asks me, clearly puzzled.

"I named the vibrator Redman. It's red and I..." my face flushes and I shut up as the embarrassment sets in. I'm telling this man all my business and I don't know him from squat.

"I get it." He looks down, trying not to grin in my face. After a moment of composing his face, he looks me directly in the eyes and says, "Analisa, look. I dig you and I think you kind of dig me. Let's hang out and see where things go from there."

I gulp air. "Well...I..."

"Don't have anything else to do. If you did, you wouldn't be sexing your vibrator. What do you say?"

This hunk of a man overwhelms me. I'm excited and nervous, but I want to get closer to this brother. What can it hurt? He just wants to spend some time getting to know me.

"All right. Let's do it. What time?"

"What are you doing now?

"Now?"

"Now. Times wasting. Get your purse and let's fly."

This brother really takes charge. I consider the idea, dismiss it and reconsider it. Before I can change my mind again, I hop off the couch, grab my purse and we are out of the door in a flash.

"My Black Knight come alive!" Travesteen screams. "Now *that's* how a real man acts—helps a female out in distress."

"Shhhht. I say out of the frying pan and into the fire. She doesn't even know him. Don't you think he's after something for himself?" Trina says with a you-are-so-slow roll of her eyes. "Now, the average man ain't gonna *help out* just to help out. They don't want to be caught up in no drama they don't have any interest in. I say he's trying to get the drawers. He's already calling her his woman, so it means he's after the cookie."

"It does not. He was probably only joking," I speak up. Trina is just too jaded about life for me sometimes. "Every once in a while, people help each other out because they should. Not for some payback down the road...because it's the right thing to do."

"Yeah, Trina, how many times have you been in a situation where you were just praying somebody would walk in or flex a little muscle letting you at least know they *might* have your back if something went down?" Cherise spits out and pushes a potato chip between her lips.

"Never! I don't expect anybody to do *shit* for me they don't have too. That's the main reason why I pack some type of protection wherever I go. I ain't laying down for no bullshit! I come ready to play!" Trina says with attitude before taking a gulp of her drink.

"Girl, a gun or a knife won't do you a bit of good if they blindside you. Most folks don't just say 'I'm gonna beat your ass'… they just *do* it." Cherise pushes her hair from her forehead.

Trina pulls her lips from her glass. "They might get a good sucker punch in one time, but I plan to be all up in their ass after that! It ain't gonna be like they thought it was!"

"You ever had your ass whipped by your significant other?" Cherise probes. Trina looks at her, then studies her glass. When no answer is forthcoming, she continues, "And you never even knew what you were all up in fray about, did you? They're smiling one second, then POW! and the next thing you know, you're eating the carpet and trying to get some relief from the kicks or punches and stuff. A gun ain't no protection against an ambush. Shoot. I think saving my life might be worth a little slice of coochie."

We all remain silent, musing over some violent past hurt or another.

"You know, it doesn't seem like people were so mad a few years ago like they are today. Any little thing sets them off— your makeup, the color of your clothes— anything," Travesteen speaks quietly.

"Travesteen, there's always been domestic violence. The only difference is people didn't let you know it. Many a woman, or man, for that matter, has been slapped, kicked and raped by somebody who supposedly loved them. It's nothing new. It's just become news," I point out.

"Yeah, but the only ones they're really concerned about are the heterosexual relationships. Let a gay man beat up or rape his boyfriend and what happens? Nothing. Just like for lesbians— absolutely nothing. It's a joke to them. 'That faggot got his or her ass whipped. Shouldn't have been fucking like that anyway.' All a big joke!" Cherise fairly shouts.

"Cherise, we all know it's not right how they treat gay people," I say slowly. "I think they really don't know *what* to do in those situations. I mean, homophobia is in every heterosexual person in the world. They'd be lying if they said it wasn't. The greatest fear a straight person has is they will be raped or something by somebody of the same sex. So, I guess when they are actually faced with these situations, they just don't *know* the correct way to act. All their own prejudices and misconceptions drive their actions. Not conscience correctness. Subconscious reaction."

"But, they act like we're second class citizens or something. It just hurts." I see the tears threatening in Cherise's eyes.

Trina better not make a lesbian comment here!

"Cherise, we all love you, gay or not." Travesteen says soothingly and pats her arm. "I know it's a difficult situation, or I think so anyway, but just know we care about you and we'll help you in whatever."

"I know you all will, it's the other folks I'm concerned about. Don't worry Trina, I know you don't feel that way." Cherise stares at Trina.

I hold my breath waiting for Trina to reply.

"Girl, I'm just playing with you and stuff. You know I like you. I'll defend your dyke ass in a minute!" Trina says before bursting out in laughter.

"You are stupid! Let's get back to the story. We seemed to have gotten off track with the domestic violence scene and all." I retrieve the manuscript and begin Chapter Four.

CHAPTER 4

I squeal when I see the restored 1964 Mustang convertible Chance leads me to. I had always dreamed of owning one ever since I saw my first back in Mississippi. It wasn't nearly as nice as the one Chance has, but so what? I can hardly contain myself as I slip into the seat, bouncing up and down like a pre-schooler.

"Put the top down!" I say happily as he settles into the car.

"Won't it mess up your hair?" He looks at my head.

"I'm not one of those women who cares about their hair more than having some fun. So, let's put the top down so the wind can whip all through it."

"What the lady wants, the lady gets."

"Always?" I say, feeling bold enough to flirt with him.

"Pretty much," he says as he exits the car. We team up and quickly fold the top back.

As I hop back into my seat, I can't believe my good luck—riding with a sexy man, in a sexy car, and the wind whipping through my hair. What could be better?

"What would you like to do?" Chance says with a smile playing at his mouth.

"Oh, something different. I don't really want to go to the movies or the park. I want to do something I've never done before."

"Like?"

"I don't know really. I've been here nearly a year and all I ever do is go to the movies or the mall or the park. Oh, I've been to a few clubs, but I get tired of trying to avoid the men I got all dressed up to attract in the first place."

"I feel ya."

"So, I guess I'll leave it up to you. All I ask is let be something I wouldn't normally do."

"Any restrictions?"

I decide to be bodacious here, besides, I may never get another opportunity like this. I look him directly in the face and say, "None at all."

He smiles again. "Hold onto your seat girl, I've got something in mind I know you will remember forever."

He quickly does a U-turn and heads back towards the downtown area. I can't imagine what could be going on down here since everything is usually closed on Saturday.

After fifteen minutes, we pass through the main downtown streets and the area changes from the freshness you see in the brochures, to a seedy look. The smog of the city seems to have settled here—the streets are dirty; trash blows down the sidewalk. What stores there are are close on each other—paint peeling, homemade signs hung askance. The people strolling the street are multicultural and definitely not of the "white collar" working class.

As we stop for a light, my eyes bug as I watch a woman on a corner, wearing only a G-string and a bra, approach a stopped car. After a brief conversation, in which her laughing exposes more gold in her mouth than I possess in my jewelry box, she opens the car door. When she gets into the car, I turn to Chance.

"Did you see that?" I ask incredulously.

"Just wait, it gets better," he says with a wink.

I get the urge to raise the top and lock the door, ensuring my safety. Here I am with a man I don't really know, going someplace I have no idea of and nobody knows where I am or who I am with.

Am I crazy?

Chance must have read my mind because he looks at me and says, "Relax. You're safe."

As we continue on this odyssey, I try to make an effort to unclench my jaw and appear carefree. The streets whiz by and the neighborhood changes to an industrialized area. Warehouses loom and I can smell the ocean.

"Are we close?" I ask, as we navigate yet one more alley between buildings.

"Very. It will just be a few more minutes."

He swings into the parking area of a large warehouse within a minute or two and stops. I notice the lot is full even on a Saturday. *Wonder what's going on?*

"This is it," he says and steps out of the car. I sit in the car wondering what I'm about to see and really hoping I don't run out of wherever we are going screaming my head off.

"This is...safe?" I ask, as Chance lifts the ragtop into place.

"Girl, you're with me and I won't let anything you don't want happen to you. Trust me." I hardly know him, but the way he says this makes me feel certain I can trust him.

I gather all my courage and step out of the car. After making sure my purse was well hidden, Chance takes my hand and leads me to a doorway on the side of the building and knocks.

The door is immediately opened and music blasts out. A large, beefy man nearly Chance's height, looks us up and down, then ushers us inside.

The hallway is bright and the music is thumping. As Chance pays the cover charge, I notice another door just down the hall which has ENTER painted on it in gold lettering. I move slowly, tentatively, as I feel Chance's hand in the small of my back urging me forward. As my hand rests on the doorknob and I feel the vibrations of the music, he whispers in my ear, "Don't be shocked at what you see. Just go with the flow. And remember, I will *always* be by your side. *Always.*"

My heartbeat speeds up a notch at this profound statement. Just what is waiting behind the door? A wild disco? A strip joint? A gay bar? Before I can turn on my heels and run, Chance pushes the door open.

The chirping of a phone interrupts me. Cherise rises quickly.

"Do you want us to wait until you finish your call or just go on?" I ask a little irritably. *I want to know what is behind the door!*

"Hold up. It's not gonna take but just a minute," she says, staring at the LED readout. Putting the phone quickly to her mouth she says, "Hey, what's up?"

"Probably her girlfriend," Trina snorts as Cherise walk away.

"Hush," I admonish her. I sure hope whoever she is talking to finishes quickly.

Snippets of conversation drift back to us.

"...no, I didn't talk to her." Cherise listens.

"—well, she's just lying. I was at home last night. Didn't you call me from work?" Cherise has her hands in her hair as she leans on the front door.

"Something's going down!" Trina rubs her hands together before lowering her voice. "You don't suppose old Cherise is cheating on her girlfriend, do you? Shit, is it still called cheating when lesbians sleep around with other lesbians?"

"I don't *know*," I whisper back. I suppose it's called cheating when you step on your significant other, male or female, but we didn't even know who she was talking to.

All eyes are riveted as Cherise suddenly yells, "This is shit! Just shit! I just *told you* and you still don't believe me!"

"Uhmmm. I think the mess has hit the fan, whatever it is," Travesteen whispers.

"You think so?" Trina says with a smirk.

"Quit. She could be talking about something going down at school. We don't know if Cherise is even in a relationship right now. It's not like we've ever seen her with her lovers." I interject while watching Cherise closely. Whatever it was, I didn't plan to miss nary moment of it.

"I'm glad too. The last thing I want to see is two lesbos hugged up. Thinking about that shit is about to make me throw up." Trina makes a face.

We try to giggle quietly, hands over our mouths, but Cherise takes this moment to blurt out something ridiculous.

"Well, screw you and the pussy that had you too!" She shouts before clicking off.

Our giggles turn into loud, hooting laughter. We try to staunch the laughter as Cherise walks back over to us, but fail.

"What the hell is so funny?" She stands over us, arms on her hips.

"I never thought I would ever ask another woman this but...woman problems?" Trina says between laughs.

We crack up even harder.

"Y'all make me sick." Cherise says before she begins giggling herself.

"Who were you talking to anyway?" I venture to ask between gulps of air.

"You don't even want to know," Cherise replies.

"Believe me, we *do*." Travesteen says gleefully.

"Yeah," I chime in. "I'm like the kids now. What's the 4-1-1?"

Cherise shakes her head.

"Come *on*. You can't tell us nothing we haven't heard before…I guess you can't anyway," Trina blurts out.

Cherise hiccups before she begins. "That was Sonia. My girlfriend." Trina raises her eyebrows and gives me an I-told-you-so look. "She called to tell me her friend, Liz, said she saw me with some other woman last night at the club. Just silly shit." Cherise waves her hands at us like that pitiful explanation was good enough.

"Were you?" Trina asks the question which was about to burst from my mouth.

"Was I what?" Cherise has the audacity to look perplexed. She knows what the hell we want to hear!

"Were you at the club with some other woman?" I screech, filling in the blanks that weren't even present.

Cherise is quiet.

"Go on and tell us. It's not like we're gonna go out and try to steal her from you, you know." Trina grimaces at the thought. I try to quell a laugh but fail.

"Well…" Cherise begins and stops.

"What?!" Travesteen yells after a few moments.

"Alright." Cherise takes a deep breath and begins reluctantly. "Yes. I was talking to a woman at the club."

Trina hollers at this news. "Girl, now who's the 'ho?"

"Hold up, Trina. Let her finish." I respond, wanting to get the dirt.

"It's not like what you're thinking. We just had a few drinks and talked a while…" Cherise tries to explain.

"How long is 'a while?'" Travesteen interrupts.

Cherise looks at her a moment before replying, a smile on her lips. "Until three o'clock in the morning."

"Hoooo! Girl, you were *cheating* on Sonia!" I laugh. "Three o'clock."

"Was not. Conversation is *not* cheating," Cherise asserts.

"And bumping monkeys is not sex, but who's counting." Trina shakes her head. "A lesbian 'ho. Who would have ever thought it?"

"I am not a whore just because I *talked* to another woman," Cherise insists.

"Okay. Is the term lesbian *dog* more appropriate? That's an oxymoron, isn't it, Travesteen?" Trina looks Travesteen's way.

"Something like that...but dog is really a *harsh* word." Travesteen says while trying to control the laughter bubbling in her throat.

"Let's change the subject." Cherise waves her hands at me, brushing the comment off. "Why don't we get back to the story? Where were you Zay?"

"You sure? We kind of like your story right now." I say, interested in the specifics of what happened last night, or rather this morning.

"Well, that chapter is finished, so let's just read." Cherise looks at me, her eyes imploring me to open the manuscript. I can't, though.

"Are you *really* sure? We can psychoanalyze for a few more minutes on your sit-chi-ation." Trina says smugly.

"If I need psychoanalyzing, I'll get an appointment with a shrink." Cherise purses her lips.

"They got shrinks for gay folks?" Trina looks at us in feigned wonder.

Enough of this. I clap my hands. "Okay, everybody, let's just get back to the story line." I say, opening the manuscript, refusing to reply to Trina's question.

"Girl, you should write a book about your jacked up life. I can give you a title...*Butch Does Biloxi!*" Trina squeaks out and everybody but Cherise laughs hard.

"Now, that was wrong, Trina," Travesteen says with a grin on her face.

"Might be, but true," Trina replies.

"Did I tell y'all, y'all make me sick?" Cherise says, arms crossed, a petulant look on her face.

"You did," I assure her and pat her leg. "Now...back to the story."

The room we enter is dark and the music is not as loud as in the hallway. As my eyes adjust to the darkness, I see a good number of couples sitting at tables, talking in hushed tones. Good, it's couples, but no one is dancing.

My eyes are drawn to a stage lighted by one spotlight. On this stage, I see one fully clothed woman lying on a bed made of animal skins, writhing around as if she is in pain.

Oh my goodness, this isn't some Satanic stuff is it?

I look around the room, but no one looks the least bit uncomfortable so I try to relax. Chance finds a table near the front of the room and holds out my chair. A waitress ambles over and he orders two Singapore Slings.

As I look back at the stage, the woman slowly begins removing her blouse revealing a bra with no cups. Her nipples stand at attention and she moans and tweaks them with her hands. She is thrashing around; her mouth open in ecstasy.

I am intrigued. I've never ever seen another woman enjoying herself before. As I look at Chance, he smiles, reaches out and holds my hand.

I turn my attention back to the stage as the woman unzips her pants and slides them down. She turns her back to the audience and reveals panties with the material missing over her buttocks. She rubs each golden moon slowly before lying back on the skins. Her hands delve into her panties, thrusting with purpose; her mouth in a silent "O."

Chance begins a slow circular movement on my palm with his fingers. My panties moisten as I continue to watch and feel his fingers in my palm.

A second spotlight is clicked on. A man enters the stage wearing only a loincloth. As brown as she is gold, he has a well formed chest, a small waist and muscular thighs. He walks quickly to the woman and takes her into his arms, his tongue hanging out of his mouth as he lowers his face to hers. I see the workings of the muscles in his jaw and I can imagine how it must feel with him swirling his tongue around and around in the woman's mouth.

I shift in my seat trying to slow the moisture I feel beginning to creep between my lips. Chance moves his chair closer to mine and pulls me into a slight embrace—his arms resting around my shoulder, our faces touching.

The man licks the woman face. Really *licks* it, like a dog lapping at its master's face. I can see the shine of the saliva trail in the glare of the lights. The woman's tongue reaches out to meet his licking one and they entangle.

Intertwine.

I'm starting to feel warm. I want to fan my face but I don't want to be so obvious. The other couples are quietly sipping drinks and watching the stage. I notice no one is making *any* conversation now. All attention is on the show.

The woman pulls at the loincloth, permitting a glimpse of what appears to be spectacular manhood. With urgency, she pushes the thin material down, allowing the entire appendage to be revealed.

I gasp involuntarily.

I've never seen anyone built like this!

This man is probably twelve inches erect; his sac like two oranges covered by flesh. My past relationships resemble prepubescent males compared to him.

"Did you say twelve inches?" Travesteen asks, eyes wide.

"That's what is says here," I reply, looking back at the paragraph for reference, but annoyed she always seemed to interrupt whenever things were getting good.

"Damn! Chick got a monster down there, doesn't she?" Trina says with amusement.

"Y'all, hush up!" I moan, stopping any more discussion before it got started. "I've *got* to see what happens next. Here goes..."

Along with his muscular torso, he looks like a proud emperor. No bashfulness whatsoever. Just proud. And he *should* be proud.

The woman grabs hold of his member and without any preamble presses her lips around the tip of it. As she begins to work hungrily up and down his shaft, he leans his head back and opens his mouth.

Feeling it.

Absorbing it.

Suddenly, he grabs two fistfuls of her hair and begins pushing and pulling, guiding her mouth as he thrusts inwards and outwards. My eyes are glued to her mouth as it stretches and slurps. Mentally, I change places with her.

Chance begins to blow on my neck, his hands encircling my waist, pulling me tighter. I relax into his chest; head nestled in the crook of his neck. My leg, which twitches uncontrollably when I am nervous or excited, begins rapidly moving up and down. I place a hand on my knee to stop the motions, to no avail.

With effort showing on his face, the man removes the woman's lips from his shaft, drops to his knees and begins suckling her. When the woman moans, I almost moan with her. Oh, the way he is nuzzling her! I can see him tugging on the nipples, lifting each one with his teeth; the woman's fingers splayed in his hair.

Chance must be digging the scene too, because he pulls me onto his lap and seats me in front of him. I shock myself by not resisting as I feel his manhood pressing into my back.

Pulsing. Pushing.

Surprising myself further, I press backwards, feeling him more fully.

The man on the stage moves lower, spreads the woman wide, and pushes his face into her heat. I can tell by the way he is moving his head, he is *definitely* a connoisseur of Eden.

I am so aroused by this sight, the silent moan in my head is almost released. My juices are running freely; my panties a soaking mess. I wiggle my hips without regard for any consequences, allowing Chance to press into my crevice. His hands roam over my chest, my hands on top of his, guiding him to my sensitive areas.

You playing with fire, girl, the voice in my head tells me, but I am powerless to stop.

Intrigued, I watch as the man lifts his face, places his hands beneath the woman's knees and pulls her roughly towards him. He sights her opening and thrusts forward. As he is thrusting on the stage, I begin undulating back and forth in my seat. Chance undulates with me. The pace quickens and my undulating gets faster until I feel like I'm about to explode. I try to turn and face Chance, but he holds me tight and undulates into my crevice; making love through our clothes, his hands on my crotch rubbing at my center.

The man on the stage is really pumping now and the woman is arching to meet his every stroke; stoking him with circular motions and fisted hands. Just as I think I can't take it any more, with one final thrust, he removes his member and his love flows onto her stomach, pooling onto the stage. He collapses onto her and the stage goes black.

I'm still wiggling on Chance. Pushing him; feeling him push back. I don't know what to do now. I feel as though I could strip and love him right here on the table.

Chance suddenly grabs the seat of my jeans firmly, his fingers pressing on my nub. As I gasp from the sensation, I feel the zinging sensation begin in my legs and rapidly move up towards where his hands are grabbing me. I whimper and buck as the tingling reaches my nub. Chance continues grabbing and pressing on this sensitized flesh, causing the waves of completion to wash over me again and again…

Feeling drained, I slump my head onto the table. For a few minutes, Chance rubs my back; soft kisses following his hands.

"Ready to go?" he asks me quietly.

"Yeah, let's get out of here," I say shakily. After what I've just seen, I definitely *need* to get to my apartment.

"Ladies, I've got to take a break here." I say, crossing my legs, trying to hide my grinding pelvis. "I can't speak for anybody else, but this book is working for me! Let me get some Kool-Aid before I ignite!"

"Bring me some, too. Hot as this book is, I can't be drinking Jack. I'll have a stroke!" Trina says as she sets her drink down.

"Do y'all really believe they have a club like that?" Travesteen inquires.

"Hell, yeah! Girl, if I didn't know better, I would swear they were describing the Split & Lick. You know, the club they busted a year or so ago? They say this kind of stuff was going on there," Trina nods.

"I haven't heard about the Split & Lick before. You sure you weren't up in there?" Cherise asks Trina. Before she lets her answer, she says "Go on, admit it. You went there before. Did you go with a man or were you the *entertainment?*"

"You are so silly. In my line of work, I hear about all kinds of wild and crazy things. Let me clarify the situation for your *monkey-licking ass*," Trina says snidely. "I heard about the going ons in detail because some of the men in the club when they busted it, were married. Well, probably most of them were. Anyway, their wives came to see me after the big bust *because* I'm a divorce lawyer and they were considering divorce behind this mess. You dig?"

"Yeah, right," Cherise says with lips pursed.

"Were the husbands up on stage or just sitting around drinking? I mean, I can understand why performing in public would be wrong but…they won't arrest you because you're just *watching* somebody else have sex, will they?" Travesteen inquires, her eyes big as buttons. "That should be legal."

"Well, maybe in Nevada or California somewhere, but here in good old Mississippi, it's considered obscene, immoral and pornographic, therefore illegal." I answer as I walk back into the room.

"You mean I've got to go all the way to Nevada or California to see a sex show and not get arrested?" Travesteen asks incredulously.

"Or you can rent a tape," Cherise replies helpfully. "Seeing it live might be a crime, but renting a tape...you can do that all day, if you want."

"Seems like double standards, doesn't it? Being there with the action breaks the law, but if they tape it, they can legally sell it all over the street as long as everybody is over eighteen," I say, handing Trina her glass of Kool-Aid.

"That's not right. Shoot, if an adult wants to watch other adults having...sex, then they should be able too," Travesteen pouts.

"Like I said, rent a tape and you are safe," Cherise says. "Zay, you cooled off, or do you want somebody else to read?"

"I'm cool. I'm cool." I say, not feeling the least bit cool. "Let's just see what else they've got in store for us." Grabbing the manuscript, I lean back and begin again.

•

On unsteady legs, I rise and wind my way around the tables and back to the Mustang. As I reach the car and open the door, my legs finally give way and I collapse onto the seat. My arms feel like macaroni—limp, pliable. Chance notices my weakness and reaches over me and closes the door.

Retracing our route, the wind whips over my skin; heightening my lingering tingling. Goosebumps rise on my body irrespective of the hot sun burning down on me. I lay my head back and stare at the sky. Slowly, I rub my arms and legs, remembering the scenes I'd witnessed; remembering the feelings I felt.

The apartment building looms quickly before us, much quicker than our exit from it. Chance quickly finds a parking space, shuts off the engine and turns to me.

"Where do we go from here?" he asks.

I want this man. Bad. I want to feel his hands on me without the barriers of our clothes; his lips bruising mine with abandon.

Looking him directly in the eyes, I say, "Up."

With tender fingers, he gathers my face and kisses me, gently at first, then with breathless urgency, my teeth nipping at his lips; his tongue bathing me with his saliva. As the fire builds in my body, my hands roam freely on his head, his face, and his chest. Finally, the kiss is broken and I scramble to find my purse, rushing to get into *one* of our apartments.

As I walk ahead of him in the stairwell, I feel his hands slide beneath the strings of my halter, strumming my nerves. On the landing before my floor, Chance pulls the lower strings and unties the knot. My breasts, released from a minimum security prison as it was, now jiggle with each step; the thrill of knowing that all it would take was a strong gust of wind, and I would be exposed for anyone walking by to see.

So, so naughty.

I pick up the pace and my breast jiggling does also. Chance pulls on the halter strings to slow me down, clearly outlining my erect nipples through the stretched fabric.

Keys are placed in the lock and the door swings open. Without even taking a moment to close it, we are in each other's arms. Lips fused, hands searching for something and everything. He presses me against the wall, shuts the door with his foot, and begins a slow grind into my liquid body.

His grinding makes my body rise to the occasion and reciprocate. My legs spread wider and wider, allowing him to fit snugly into my crotch. My hands grasp muscular hips and pull him closer, tighter.

His teeth pull at the skin of my neck. I briefly contemplate the ugliness of a hickey, but the thought leaves as he bites into my shoulder. He nips across my collarbone to the other side of my neck. His large hands envelop my aroused breasts, lightly pinching the swollen aureoles, causing them to swell in size.

The halter has become wrapped uncomfortably around my neck. I remove it and fling it across the room where it rests on a lampshade. Chance begins plundering my breasts. His tongue and teeth flicking over, around, up and down. My toes curl from his ministrations; my grinding increasing in intensity.

The voice in my head tells me to slow down, but Chance's attention to the details forming my unique body, makes me ignore it. I want this man inside of me.

Today.

Now.

My hands grab at the waistband of his shorts and I slip my hands inside and push them downwards. Just as the shorts clear his hips, my hands begin to explore his rigidness. Rubbing and cupping, I visualize in my mind what I have yet to see and am pleased.

Chance opens my jeans and slowly glides two fingers into the waist of my panties. As his fingers are replaced by his entire hand, I tilt my mound upwards; allow him access the center of my crotch. Fingers like feathers stroke my center, release my nectar. The fit of his hands inside of panties while I'm still in jeans, is tight—his hands imprisoned; my body unable to retreat. The sensations build and build until the bubble I'm floating on finally pops.

I feel myself falling into a yawning chasm with no bottom. The synapses in my brain firing overtime, riding me onwards to the depths of pleasure. My cry being absorbed by Chance's mouth; his hands the messengers of good feelings. I slide down into myself, reeling and spinning, until the sensations finally abate...

•

Sweat is prominent on my forehead and arms. My hips continue to roll to fingers continuing to stroke.

"Chance." As he lifts his head, I see the smoky half-lidded eyes, smoldering with unfulfilled need. "Let's go to the bedroom."

Removing his hand from my pants, I grab fingers, still slick with me, and walk towards the bedroom. His free hand continues playing with my heavy breasts as we travel down the hallway.

The evening sun bathes the bedroom in shadows. I pause to pull the sheers, this time not wanting to share my soon-to-come experience with the world. My attention turns to the bed still unmade from this morning, "Redman" in clear view. I watch Chance's reaction as he lifts the vibrator and studies it.

"So this is Redman?" He asks, already knowing the answer to his question.

"That's it," I respond.

"You mind?" As I shake my head, he turns the dial at the bottom and Redman comes to life, undulating and vibrating in his hands. His hands rub over and around the vibrator, causing my body to throb with anticipation.

"Come here." A command.

My legs move on their own accord and bring me to his side in a second. Holding Redman in one hand, his lips fasten on the breast placed just at the level of his face. He pulls deeply, allowing the invisible string connecting my breasts and nub to be drawn taunt. I lean into his succulent lips, giving him free access to all of my chest.

Chance places the vibrator on the opposite breast, slowly moving from the bottom to the center of my nipple. The vibrations make my "nervous" knee shake uncontrollably. I close my eyes and collapse onto his face, forcing him to lay back on the bed, tongue and teeth in constant contact with my flesh.

My fingers tangle in the rough chest hair, my rings snagging on the fabric of the jersey. In exasperation, I roughly pull the jersey upwards and over his head, temporarily disengaging his lips from my breast. Chance quickly resume his ministrations and I feel my body responding to every nuance of his lips and the vibrations of Redman.

Fingers move the vibrator along my abdomen and sides, resting on the smooth skin between my navel and panty line. Quick, fluttery kisses from soft, succulent lips follow the trail, his teeth pulling at my belly chain. My jeans are removed and I am left only in my panties.

In past relationships, I usually felt body-conscious at this point, but with this gorgeous man, I don't feel anything *but* sexy now.

As Chance watches, I pull my panties tight—the outline of my love lips prominently displayed; the moist center of my panties telling all my wants. The whoosh of breath from

Chance's lips encourages me. I place fingers in his mouth and swirl them around as he licks them. Removing my fingers, I place them into my panties and enter Eden.

My knees are involuntarily drawn upwards as slick juices engulf my fingers, aiding my movements. Chance removes my panties, shifts my legs apart and watches enthralled as I show him my hidden world. My fingers flow upwards towards my nub and just as quickly return to my love center. On one of my return trips to Eden, Chance places the vibrating wand on my nub, moving slowly and lightly.

A fire catches quickly in my center and I move my fingers with urgency. Keeping the vibrator on my nub, Chance's fingers join mine, filling my channel. His rapid breathing telling me in a thousand words what he has not voiced.

Redman replaces our fingers and the vibrations radiate outwards to the rest of my body. *Yes.* I meet each push of the vibrator with a fervor, contracting my muscles to allow every ridge, every knob to be intensely felt as it enters and retreats.

Soon, I am welcoming the prickles as they move from my legs to my nub and center, bathing me in a two-person force field of electricity. My cries increase in volume as Chance places his lips around my twitching nub, causing my hips to buck and him to grip me tighter.

Riding the mound bull.

Taming it with his tongue...

"Shit! Call me what you want to, but Zay, you've *got* to get this brotha's number! I have some eggs he needs to fertilize!" Trina spits out while flapping the opening to her blouse.

"Brother has some skills, doesn't he?" I ask, thinking maybe I ought to see if this Sydney person really *does* know him.

"Uh hum. I wish any one of my husbands had acted like him," Travesteen says wistfully. "Maybe then we could have worked something out."

"Girl, you don't stay with no man because of sex!" Cherise snorts.

"Shut up, Cherise. You don't have a clue to how good a dick is, so just shut...up!" Trina barks.

"How do you know I hadn't had a *penis* before?" Cherise draws her eyebrows upwards.

"Shit, it's evident. If you'd had some good, stroking *penis* you wouldn't be bumping coochies in frustration. You're the one who doesn't know what you're missing," Trina states with finality.

"Well, maybe with the vibrator they use—y'all do use one, right?— it feels like what we feel with a ...you know," Travesteen says.

"Probably close," Cherise nods.

"Uh uh. Give me the real thing. Girl, if you gonna resort to a dildo anyway, why not go for the real one?" Trina asks in disgust. "Screwing a dick and screwing a dildo is the same thing."

"Trina, it's not about having something in you, it's about the person you're with," Cherise begins, a red flush rising from her neck. "I know your trifling behind can't fathom this gay thing. I didn't *ask* to be gay, I just am. I like soft women loving me versus hard men pumping into me."

"They got some soft men that don't pump too hard!" Trina laughs. "I ain't looking for him, but maybe for you—"

"That's *your* opinion. That's not what *I* need." Cherise stands suddenly and walks towards the bathroom.

We are quiet as we watch her go.

I turn on Trina the minute the bathroom door closes. "You and your big mouth. Why are you always sweating her?" I ask, watching as Trina begins eating chips nonchalantly. "And you don't even think you're wrong, do you?"

"No," Trina replies between crunches.

"I think you offended her, Trina," Travesteen says quietly. "You should apologize when she gets back."

"Look, I don't know why y'all are all up in my soda pop, but I didn't tell her no lies. She's doing the same thing we're doing except she wants to suck on some titties in the meantime!" Trina states righteously. "Shit, if either of you were with a man and y'all were just about to get your groove on and he pulls out two or three *inches*? Don't tell me you wouldn't be disappointed. You know you would. Then, all you *could do* is rub pelvises and have him push a dildo in you to get off. Now, that's probably the closest I'll ever come to being a lesbian. Probably the only time too, 'cause when the night is over, his ass is *his*-tory!" Trina cracks up.

"You are so wrong," I say, hoping Cherise wasn't so mad she wanted to leave.

"Trina, there might be some truth in what you say, but do you have to say it like you do? There's a nice way to say anything, and I think you need to make more of an effort to do that." Travesteen states, lifting her chin while looking down her nose.

"Look, Miss Daisy, my style is to spit the shit out. All this pussyfooting and stroking of egos just isn't me. I'm sorry if she was offended, but she ought to know me by now," Trina finishes and places another chip in her mouth.

Cherise walks back into the room, eyes and nose red, and sits in her chair. She sniffs slightly before saying, "Zay, can we go on? I want to hear some more. Maybe it will make me normal. You know, *hetero*." She looks at Trina when she says this.

"Gonna take more than this story to do that." I hear Trina mumble.

"Sure." I say brightly to cover up whatever else Trina might say. "Here we go...."

•

80

In the afterglow, Chance spoons his body into mine and holds me. No pressure, no urgency, just cuddling. I wonder who is this wanton creature I have become? Why have I never responded to anyone else like this? My thoughts are interrupted as Chance asks me, "Sore?"

"Not really," I respond.

"Sure?"

"Why don't you find out?" I bait him, ready for whatever is to come.

Chance slowly turns my face towards him and rains kisses on my eyes, nose and mouth. My hands roam over his substantial maleness; stroking, squeezing the tip lightly. He quickly comes to life. Strong hands rub over soft thighs before he begins his search for my sweet center. His fingers locate the bounty and slip inside easily, as I am still moist from earlier. The fingers strum my nub and I feel the post-climatic lethargy leave my body, replaced by anticipation.

After protecting him (with my stash in the bedside table), I quickly guide him into me from behind, not needing protracted foreplay, just him inside of me. He strokes inside me slowly, methodically. His pelvis grinding into my buttocks with each thrust of his hips.

I locate Redman and switch the dial until it is just vibrating. Slowly, I roll the wand along Chance's thighs, the vibrations disseminating to me. He misses a stroke as the wand is placed on his sac, but quickly picks up the pace. His hand covers mine holding the vibrator and he guides it towards my love center.

My breath quickens as he aligns the wand parallel to him and places the tip into my center. With quick thrusts, the wand is worked inside of me along side Chance's manhood, stretching my entryway to accommodate the extra member.

The pleasure-pain is excruciatingly delicious. Cries of ecstasy flow from my lips as the pleasure of this overfulfillment encircles me.

Engulfs me.

Consumes me.

Chance is gliding into me furiously. Grunts are expelled with each thrust; his sweat drenches my back.

We move towards the stratosphere together; the sun obliterating all thought as we clear the clouds...

"Did he just put Redman in with his penis?" Cherise asks, surprise and disbelief clouding her face.

"That's right. Two of them snug-as-bug in her coochie," Trina says.

"Now, that's too much. That's like having...two *dildos* in your stuff," Cherise says incredulously.

"Girl, you hadn't had two dildos in you at one time before?" Trina pokes fun at her.

"Like you have," Cherise snorts.

"Nope." Trina pops some nuts in her mouth.

"Anyway, for your information, I have had two in me before." Cherise lowers her eyes suggestively. "They just weren't in the same...*hole*, if you know what I mean."

I spray the Kool-Aid I had just placed in my mouth over everybody.

"*Damn!*" They shout together as the Kool-Aid settles on them.

"I'm sorry. I'm sorry." I say as I rush to gather paper towels. Tearing off lengths at random, I pass them around and everyone begins mopping at their face and clothes as I beg apologies all the while.

"Zay, you all right? Did the Kool-Aid go down the wrong way?" Travesteen inquires, staring into my face.

"No. I was just so...*surprised* at what Cherise said...and it just...came out," I say, still a little flustered.

"Zay, Cherise is *gay*. That means she already does more freaky stuff than the average woman any day of the week," Trina says.

"What's freaky about it? Having a dildo in the cat and one up the butt ain't no worse than having one in the cat and sucking on one or having two in the cat." Cherise says, flinging her hair over her shoulder.

I knew Cherise was gay, but I had no idea she was a kinky internet web site come alive. *I'm definitely gonna Febreeze the hell out of that chair when she gets up!*

"Well, if you're just dealing with one man, there is no way you can be sucking and f'ing at the same time. You would have to be a freak to be able to do both 'cause then you would need *two* men," Trina explains with much neck popping.

"Trina, I've been meaning to ask you...just what is your definition of being a freak?" Travesteen asks quietly. "The last time I checked, a freak was an aberration of nature. A mutation. When I have sex any way my partner wants, am I freaky? We're supposed to please our partner just like he's supposed to please us. So, if you need two vibrators or penises in you at one time to receive pleasure, is it really being freaky? Or just asking for what you know you need?"

Uh oh. I do believe Miss Scarlett's got some skeletons in the closet with meat still on the bones!

"Yeah, Trina, is that being a freak?" Cherise smirks.

"Yep. It sho' is." Trina says. "A straight up freak."

"So, you think oral sex is freaky too?" I ask. I mean, that's a normal part of the act. It may not have been when I first started, but I can't imagine life without a little tongue lashing of the coochie kind...one man at a time, of course.

"No. I said having two dildos or dicks in you at the same time is freaky." Trina clarifies. "A brother can lick me *all* he wants."

"If you can put it in your mouth, you can put it up your butt. Neither one of them is considered the 'normal' way of having sex, so I don't see the difference!" Cherise slaps her thighs.

"That's your screwed up opinion, Butchie." Trina sets her Kool-Aid down. "I don't care what you think, but if a brother tries to put something up the crap shooter, me and him gonna have a problem."

"So...I'm not trying to pry here but I need to understand something...you are saying, all you do in the bedroom is straight sex and occasional oral?" Travesteen asks. When Trina nods she continues. "You don't want...*more* sometimes? Just straight sex has got to be boring as heck!"

"There's plenty of folks out there having just straight sex and it's good. You don't have to get all the toys and stuff for it to be good, you know." Trina rolls her eyes.

"Yeah, but those same folks have affairs and do all kinds of frea...different stuff they don't do at home." I pipe up and say.

"Uhm hum. I don't think you are being true to yourself when you say you don't want to try some of this stuff. You had to think about doing something different a time or two." Cherise looks questioningly at Trina who just shakes her head.

"Right. Like my mama always said, 'If you please your man, your man will please you.'" Travesteen smiles as she drops her bit of Mama-ism on us.

"I think you mean 'the same thing it took to get him is the same thing it takes to keep him.' If I don't do nothing freaky before we get hitched, he shouldn't expect nothing freaky from me afterwards," Trina insists, looking from one of us to the other.

"Trina, when the raggedy tape on your closet door finally breaks, we're gonna find you walking the streets wearing a G-string, fishnet pantyhose and your fur in 20 degree weather!" Cherise hollers and we all fall out laughing.

I take this opportunity to say, "Let's get back to the story!"

CHAPTER 5

I awaken with my legs imprisoned by thick thighs, an arm cradling my head, and warm breath on my face. A feeling of gloriousness fills me to my core. Glancing at the clock, I see it is after eleven.

Oh, if my mother could see me now. This wanton wild-haired woman lying in bed next to an almost stranger she's made love to with abandon. Imaging the shock on her face clears my head somewhat. Okay, maybe not.

Sighing, I slowly extricate my legs, trying not to awaken Chance. After a quick bathroom visit, I continue to the kitchen to prepare breakfast. Before I remove the sizzling bacon from the hot pan, arms encircle me from behind and a kiss is placed on my lips.

"Hmmmm. A sexy woman in the kitchen, good food smells waking me up... what more can a poor man like me want?" Chance says into my ear.

"I know. What about a sexy man putting food on the table for us to eat and cleaning up afterwards?" I ask.

"No problem. I *know* my way around a kitchen," he says with attitude.

"And that's not all you know your way around," I wink at him.

Chance fills the plates I hand him with our breakfast food and we sit down to what I hope, surprisingly, will be the first of many mornings to come.

Where did that thought come from?

Conversation is scarce as we wolf down the food. I didn't realize how hungry I was, but as I think back, it was probably yesterday at the beach, since I'd eaten anything at all. True to his word, he cleared the plates and had the kitchen spic-and-span in record time.

"What would you like to do today?" Chance asks as he sits next to me on the couch. I lean into him and align my legs along the seat.

"Oh, I don't know. What do you have in mind?"

"Well, they have an outdoors blues festival over at Sessums Park. I thought it would be a good way to pass part of the day. You like blues?"

"Do I like blues? I know *all* about blues music."

"You do?" he asks.

"Yeah. I grew up in Mississippi, home of Muddy Waters and B.B. King. All I heard was blues, blues and more blues. I'm surprised y'all listen to that here."

"They listen to *everything* here—blues, rock, rap, R&B, tehano, heavy metal—you name it and they have a station playing it." Chance eyes me suspiciously. "Mississippi. I would never have guessed you were from Mississippi."

"Why? Because I have no drawl?"

"Partly. But, you aren't what I thought a girl from Mississippi would be like."

"What did you think we would be like? Slow? Don't let the hype fool you."

"I didn't think you would be slow, just—"

"You better stop before you write a check your behind can't cash," I tell him with a laugh.

"Yeah."

"Where are you from?"

"Originally, I'm from the Cuba. My parents were able to get out before Castro shut down the country and moved first to Florida, then New York."

"Cuba? Now you don't look like any Cubans I ever met." I say, eyes skeptical.

"How many Cubans do you know?"

"I know a few. I lived in Florida for four years in design college so I met people from all over. The Cubans I met all seemed more...Hispanic. I never met any black Cubans."

"Cubans come in all colors, my lady—white, brown, gold, and black."

"How'd you get all the way across country?"

"I got a football scholarship at Cal State. When I didn't make the pro cut, I decided to stay out here anyway. I love it."

"What does pro cut mean?"

"I didn't make the team. You know, professional football team."

"Oh. So, what do you do?"

"I work for Brown, Inc. as a sport promotions manager."

"Sports promotions. Is that like an agent?"

"Not at all. I travel around the country handling contract arrangements for sporting events. We put on medium to large sporting events. Everything from arena football to kick-boxing to ice hockey."

"So are you trying to be an agent?"

"No indeed," he shakes his head emphatically. "Knowing all the athletes I know, there is no way I have the patience needed to baby them. They may be large, but a lot of them still need some mothering and I'm not cut out for that." He shakes his head. "So what do you do?"

"I'm the head fashion designer at Tylos."

"Tylos. Isn't that the place with all the funky new clothes I see the rich broads wearing?"

"One and the same."

"You say you're the head designer?"

"Yes. I have four designers working under me, but the majority of the clothes you see the women wearing, I designed myself."

"All right! Are you planning to branch out on your own?"

"In a few years. It takes a lot of money to launch a new fashion line, so I'm saving as much as I can until that day comes around."

"Do you think you will have any problems with the company when you leave? You didn't sign a non-compete agreement did you?"

"No. I came into the company as a junior designer, then when the head designer left, they liked my designs enough, they offered me her position. The only agreement I've signed was a confidentiality agreement."

"That's should make everything easier for you."

"I sure hope so."

"Let me take a look at the contract sometimes and I can tell you for sure."

"Good deal. Hey, since you are Cuban and all, do you speak Spanish?"

"Fluently."

"Say something to me."

"Uhm, let's see." Chance eyes me for a moment then says, "*¿Le gustaría bailar?*"

"And that means?"

"Would you like to dance?" he answers, a grin playing along his lips.

Surprised at the suggestion, I nonetheless, take only a moment to reply, "Yes."

Rising from the couch, I quickly locate my favorite Patti LaBelle CD. As the music from *Somewhere Over the Rainbow* fills the room, Chance pulls me into his arms. I'm surprised at his fluid movements. When I've danced with large men in the past, I usually spent more time trying to breathe since their arms are holding my head tight to their chests. Chance, however, moves his hips smoothly, swaying softly to the music. Holding my arms lightly, my body responds to his subtle directions and we dance to our own rhythm until the song finishes.

"Vámonos a algún otro sitio," he says into my ear.

"Meaning?" I say, watching his sensuous lips.

"Let's go someplace else," his hooded eyes hold me enthralled.

"Like?" My heartbeat quickens.

"Alcoba."

I don't know what he said, but it *sounded* exotic, so I say, "Yes, to whatever you just said."

"Don't you want to know?"

"Not really, but okay."

"The bedroom. Girl…I want to be inside of you again."

The meltdown starts in my feet and moves up my body, just thinking about another round of lovemaking. "You spoil all of your *friends* like this?"

"No. But, I do *my woman* like this."

Yeah, baby, that's the right answer. Quickly grabbing his hand, I lead the way towards the bedroom. Anticipation sets up a now familiar tingling in my lower body. I jump onto the bed and lay on my back. Chance leans his body over me, his lips open to welcome mine and....

BBBBRRRIIIIINNGGGGG!

The phone breaks the hypnotic contact between his eyes and mine. Darn! I fumble with the phone, dropping it once and finally placing it to my ear.

"Uh, hello?" I say breathlessly, my voice higher pitched than usual.

"Analisa?" A hesitant voice asks.

"Yes?"

"Girl, what wrong with you?" I recognize Venetra's voice.

"Hey, Venetra. What's up?" I lean away from Chance and sit up on the bed.

"Just the same old, same old. Did I catch you at a bad time?"

"No. I wasn't doing anything." Chance smiles at me, parts my robe and places his soft lips on my thighs. I inhale as his lips meet my skin.

"What are you doing, girl?"

"Nothing," I wheeze as Chance's goatee scratches my thigh. In my efforts to get away, I squirm and jostle the phone. My mind goes blank for a few moments when his teeth nip my flesh. I then realize Venetra is speaking. "What did you say?" I ask.

"I *asked* you if you had tried out the massager yet? What's wrong with you?"

Not a doggone thing. Girl, if you only knew.

I try unsuccessfully to form words to answer her question, but when Chance begins sucking my thigh, they jumble in my mind. I moan uncontrollably.

"Analisa! Analisa! What's wrong!" Venetra exclaims.

I turn my mind back to Venetra and her barely registering questions. "Wrong? Why nothing's wrong," I say too brightly, trying to focus.

"Why are you moaning, then?" Venetra asks irritated. "I thought something had happened."

Not yet, but there is a good possibility it will. Chance smiles at me and I return the smile. "I don't remember moaning," I say, distractedly.

As Chance resumes sucking my thigh, another moan escapes my lips.

"See! There you go moaning into the phone again. What in the world are you doing?"

"Nothing!" Chance's tongue begins a slow swirling dance higher on my thighs, "Ah...Venetra? Ah...what's going on?"

"Nothing, and you already *asked* me that. Analisa, are you using your massager right now or something?"

I sit straight up in the bed, dislodging Chances tongue from my thigh, "No!"

"You're doing *something* over there."

"I am *not* doing anything over here."

Venetra is quiet and I can hear the cogs in her mind working overtime, trying to come up with a reason for my actions. Chance purses his lips and crosses his eyes, making me giggle. I cover the phone with my hand to deaden the sound, but I know I am unsuccessful when Venetra says, "Analisa Mathers, do you have a *man* over there?"

"Uh...Venetra, why do you say that?"

"You haven't been able to decently answer a single question I've asked your behind and now you are giggling and I didn't tell a joke."

"It's the television. I heard something funny, that's all."

"I don't hear no television."

"I've got it down low."

"Then how'd you hear the joke? Lip reading? What show is it anyway? The way it's got you caught up, I want to watch it too."

Why does she keep riding me? "Venetra, girl let me call you back later. I've had a long day and when I wake up fully I'll give you a ring, okay?"

"Long day? Girl, it's just after 12 o'clock out there. The day is just starting."

I gulp, caught in my own shenanigans. Chance uses this opportunity to begin licking my thighs again and I forget I'm even on the phone.

"Analisa."

When I don't reply she shouts, "Analisa! I'll let you get back to your *show* that's keeping you from talking to me and I'll talk to you later," and slams the phone down.

Oh, well.

"Girls, don't we act just like that? We'll give some sexy gift, then mess up the groove we gave the gift for in the first place." I laugh since I've done exactly that.

"You ain't never lied. We'll cock-block in a minute!" Trina hoots.

"That's sure us. Venetra knows she knew what was going on. Instead of just wishing her well and hanging up, she copes an attitude. Classic woman." Cherise laughs.

"I sure hope it hasn't got her out of the mood because I want to hear more about her and Chance in the bedroom. Black, Cuban and he speaks Spanish. Ohhhh! Zay, you *need* to find out if he's real or not!" Travesteen says in anguish.

"Girl, if he is, all of us are gonna try kill each other for him!" Trina laughs and says. "We all want to be that man's baby's mama!"

"Quit." I say, flipping her the bird. To be honest, I don't want to end any friendships, but if Chance walked in the door right now, I just might be facing jail time when it's all over.

"Read, Zay!" Travesteen shouts.

I replace the phone in its cradle and arrange myself on the bed so Chance has better access to my trembling thighs. "You are so, so bad," I tell him.

"I know, and now you do too," he answers and returns to my thighs. Just as I felt his breath warming the entrance to Eden, the phone rings again.

"Ignore it," Chance says, but the ringing is persistent. Frustrated at this interruption, I pick up the phone and gruffly yell, "Hello!"

"Hey baby. How's your day going?"

Oh, goodness, it's my mother. Thinking about her earlier must have drummed her up. "It's going good, Moma."

"Not the mama again!" Travesteen moans.
"HUSH!" We all yell at her.

"That's great. Look, the reason I called is, I ran into Myra this morning and she wanted me to tell you she might, and this is only a *might*, want to have her back out in her wedding dress."

93

As I watch Chance leaning towards me, I stop him with a hand to his forehead and a NO shake of my head. While I'm talking to my mother is *not* the time for a little foreplay.

"So, she wants her back out." That ought to save about three yards of fabric right there.

I put my fingers to my lips, indicating to Chance he should stay quiet. I'm not ready for my mother to know I've got a man over here first thing in the day. That might lead to questions I don't want her to ask and I sure as heck don't want to answer.

"She says she *might.* I tried to talk to her about it a little, so I'm hoping she will take some of the things I told her to heart and forget that mess."

I hear the irritation in her voice. If nothing else, my mother believes in saving yourself for marriage and looking like a *lady*, or her definition of one anyway, at all times. As she begins speaking again, I know this might take a while.

"I tell you, you young folks do things a whole lot different than we did back when I got married. Back then, all we wanted was a sparkling white dress and a man with a good job and big dreams. Now, you jump into bed with the first man *looking* like he can give you a good time, shack before you get married and when you do get married, y'all wear any kind of color —black, red, purple—the color white don't mean nothing to y'all at all. That's probably the reason why so many of you young people stay married only a hot minute—ain't no mystery. Y'all have already showed everything you got before they get you."

"Uh…Moma?" I say trying to interrupt and end the conversation.

"I don't know what's got into Myra. She was raised right. I don't know why she would want to stand up there in front of God and everybody and show all her goodies."

Chance lifts off the bed and walks around it. I watch the muscles in his buttocks clench and squeeze as he walks. Putting my hand out, I skim the smooth flesh as moves past me towards the bathroom.

"You said she found a good man, didn't you?"

"Yeah, he *seems* like he is good, but he might get a different idea once he sees his new bride coming down the aisle looking like a Las Vegas showgirl."

"Moma, quit exaggerating."

"I'm not exaggerating! What else do you call it when a woman come down the aisle with her dress open to the crack in her back? And on her wedding day, no less."

"I would call it daring."

"Yes, I guess you would. I remember all those clothes you use to make around here—splits to your cookie, half your boobs falling out—if I didn't try to raise you right, I would have let you wear all them clothes. But, I *knew* those kind of clothes weren't nothing but trouble."

"Moma, I didn't wear any clothes like that!" I say, annoyed at her suggestion.

"You sure didn't, because I stopped you. Now it looks like your tastes have spilled over to other folks in the family." She is in a tizzy now.

"Moma, I'll talk to Myra. Maybe I can design something with just a little of her back out, like a diamond cutout covered with lace or something."

"Maybe...I don't know. It just doesn't seem right, though."

You telling me! Big Myra with her back exposed, her *at minimum,* four rows of flab exposed for everyone to see. I almost gag at the vision.

"Let me work at designing something slimming with a sexy back view for her to look at."

"You ain't *supposed* to be sexy at your wedding. You supposed to look like you hadn't had any before."

"Well, Moma, as you said, our generation does things a little different from yours."

"You've got that right." I hear her mumble about girls wearing gasoline drawers or something then she says, "Did you try out the massager on those sore muscles yet?"

Her changing gears caught me by surprise and I stutter, "N...not really." It's not a lie. I *didn't* use the massager on my sore legs.

"What are you waiting on? Weren't your feet and legs aching from standing all day when I talked to you Friday?"

"Yes, just a little."

"Well then, why didn't you use the massager? Chile, if someone gives you something you need at the moment you need it, count it as a blessing and *use* it!"

It sure was a blessing in disguise. The pleasure that little massager has brought me has been indescribably delicious. "I will," I say.

"Well, the next time I call, I'm expecting to get an update on how the massager is working for you, all right?"

"All right, Moma."

"Moma loves you. Bye now."

"Bye."

Well that long speech sure cooled my body down immensely. No matter, I can get back in the swing of things with just a little help. I hang up the phone and I am surprised as Chance walks out of the bathroom fully clothed.

"Where are you going?" Here he is fully clothed and I'm thinking we could get started on a long day of lovemaking.

"I'm just going to head over to my apartment, take care of a few things, grab a shower and I'll meet you back here later. What, an hour or two?"

Relief floods through me. For a minute, I thought he was going to turn out to be one of those men who just want to "hit it and quit it." I turn on a megawatt smile. "That's fine. I'll grab a shower and a nap but I'll be ready when you get here."

With a quick kiss to my lips and warm hands brushing over my bare chest, he walks to the door and leaves. I lay back on the bed, close my eyes and revel in the awakened feelings now zinging through my body.

My, my, my. I spend an entire year trying to meet someone exciting, with no luck, and all of a sudden, excitement just shows up at my door.

I drift off to sleep reliving the tag-teaming of Chance and Redman in my mind, my body flushing desire…

"Now, speak." I say as I finish the chapter.

"That mama needs to quit interfering!" Travesteen says first. "She acts just like mine—calling and messing up a perfectly good make-out session."

"Make-out session? That's what y'all call it where you come from?" Cherise asks.

"Yeah. Some folks call it other things, but we call it making out."

"In Jackson, we called it 'doing the nasty,'" Trina flips. "Most of the time, we called it fu—"

"No you don't! We're striking that word from here tonight!" I shout at her. "This story is not about the "f" word, it's about making love."

"They don't even know each other! You don't call sleeping with somebody on the first date making love." Trina rolls her eyes. "Where I come from, we call that fu—"

"Hush!" I yell, cutting her off. "You're trying to make this story into a trashy novel and it's not." I take a deep breath. "Now, I'm gonna speak from experience here. I've met people I clicked with and we had us a good time *on the first date*. We just sparked and getting together felt right. I don't recommend it today, but if you ever have had an experience like that...you won't forget it."

"You weren't scared he would do something to you like rape you or kill you?" Travesteen inquires.

"No. I felt just like she did—safe and...*horny!*" I finish, laughing.

"You right! Your ass was just horny!" Trina laughs with me.

"I feel ya, Zay. I've wanted to do things with a new friend but I just never followed through with it. Something about my upbringing, I guess. Anyway, I definitely missed the moment on a number of occasions," Cherise adds.

"You mean to tell me lesbians don't just signal each other, go to an apartment and bump monkeys? Even on the first date? That's hard to believe." Trina lifts her eyebrows.

"That's right. We actually *do* take the time to date before we get to rolling around in the sheets together," Cherise sneers.

"Ain't that something?" Trina looks at Travesteen and myself. "You learn something new every day."

"And if anybody up in here needs to learn something, it's *you*," Cherise smarts back.

"Now, don't y'all start." Travesteen shakes her head.

Trina flicks her hand at her.

"Zay, take a break and let me read," Cherise says, holding out her hand for the manuscript.

"Well...I...uh..." I stammer because I don't want to give up the book I'm holding.

"You're starting to sound tired, so I'll read now." Cherise has decided to walk over and *pry* the papers out of my hand. With reluctance, my fingers release the manuscript and Cherise settles back in her seat. "Where were you? Oh, I see it. Now..."

CHAPTER 6

I awaken and realize I had been asleep for nearly an hour. I stretch slowly, like a cat, then pad over to the sliding door and peer through the sheers, trying to see if Chance is on his balcony. Empty. I head for the bathroom and a quick shower.

After a cooling shower, I ponder over what to wear to an outdoor concert. I pull out jeans and a shirt and discard it as too hot. A short set was nice, but I thought they might be too revealing for a second date.

Did you forget what happened after the first date, girl?

Giggling at the irony of the situation, I decide on a sexy short white denim dress. The criss-crosses at the back have drawn a number of whistles when I've worn it in the past and I'm sure it should do the trick on Chance today.

Feeling quite flirtatious, I put on a pair of thongs and pat gold skin powder on both cheeks. There. I apply a dab of makeup, spritz on my favorite perfume, then wander in the living room and plop on the chocolate sofa. I luxuriate in its softness and soon my senses dull and I drift off.

A knock on the door awakens me in a flash. After confirming it is indeed Chance, I open the door and I am immediately caught up in a huge hug.

"I missed you, girl," he says into my ear.

"You've only been gone a couple of hours," I reply.

"Yeah, but it seems like a week." Chance hugs me tighter before releasing me. He steps back, looks at me from head to toe and gives a long whistle.

This dress doesn't let me down!

"Girl, I'm scared of *you*!"

"Don't be scared. I don't bite."

"You can if you want to. Call me Cookie!" I swat at his chest and laugh with him.

"Ready?" I ask, anxious to get going.

"Ready if you are," he answers and bows.

As I walk past him, I feel his hands roaming under my skirt. The short intake of breath and exclamation of "Aw, hell!" tells me he has discovered the thongs. I pass through the door and wiggle my hips invitingly as I strut in front of him.

"Keep it up and we are going to miss everything," Chance eeks out between clenched teeth.

I turn an innocent face towards him. "What do you mean?"

"Girl, I'm about to catch on fire. Just remember, fire burns *everything* in its path until a little moisture cools it down," Chance says with meaning.

I keep the innocent look on my face. "Chance, you say the most unusual things."

"Not yet, but keep on walking like that and you might hear some things you haven't heard in a long time."

"In Spanish?" I say hopefully.

"And English." He affirms tersely.

Deciding not to entice him further, I slow down and walk beside him. Chance takes my hands, kisses each finger lightly and licks my palm. The tingling starts and I feel the humming of the muscles of my lower lips as they ready themselves. Knowing that more of this type of foreplay would lead back into my apartment, I pull my hand from his lips and walk down the stairwell.

On the first landing we reach, Chance grabs me, pulls me into the shadows and kisses me hurriedly, his hands plundering my breasts, hips, thighs.

This assault on my body awakens it fully and I respond with enthusiasm—rubbing the V of his pants and running my fingers over his back.

Rapid steps on the stairwell cause us to jump apart. We try to give the impression of a couple making light conversation before going out as a young man bounds up the stairwell and past us with a hurried, "Hey."

When the man is out of sight, Chance takes a deep breath. "You really want to go to this concert?" I watch him as he watches me, seeing the want in his eyes as his hands stroke mine.

"I want what you want." I look into his eyes.

"I want your warm, silky thighs wrapped around my back. Now, that's what I want right now. Is that what you want?"

The sudden rush of desire makes my tongue leaden, unable to mutter a single word.

"I mean...I don't want to go too...fast," Chance says, giving me an out I don't want as the estrogen surges through my system.

I smile at him. "That's my line, isn't it?"

The emotions play over Chance's face—hunger, desire and finally resignation. "Hey, let's go to the concert. We'll take it slow, for now, and later..."

I smile again. "Yeah, later," I say with promise in my voice. I tighten my hands around him and we continue to the car.

"Damn the concert! Me and Chance need to get a little better acquainted!" Trina yells. "She is a fool! I'd have his ass in a thigh-lock by now."

"I have to say it does sound like maybe they could put the concert off...you know, work on developing the *relationship* more," Travesteen nods.

"Girl, you just want to hear about the sex," Cherise tells her.

"Yes, I do. Especially since they are doing some things I haven't tried out just yet," Travesteen replies.

"I'll bet. You've had four husbands so you need to stop acting so prim. You know your coochie's been around the block a few times." Trina plucks her arm. "It's a wonder your uterus doesn't fall out."

"I'll have you know my coochie is as tight as a young girls," Travesteen says and winks.

" Waaaa..." I fall back in laughter.

"That's not saying much. Shoot, most young girls nowadays know and do way more than we ever did," Cherise interjects.

"Now, Cherise, most girls don't go around looking up in other girl's coochies." Trina crosses her arms.

"You know what she meant, Trina." I swat at her. "If I'd of acted like some of these girls do today, I believe my stuff would be big enough to drive a tractor-trailer through it."

"Not me. I do my Kegels *every* night," Travesteen says proudly, referring to the exercises which are supposed to tighten up your pelvic muscles.

"Does it work?" Cherise inquires, laughter in her eyes.

"It sure does," she answers. "My last husband said he thought he was screwing a sixteen-year-old virgin."

"Damn! That ain't no compliment. He was a pervert! What's a grown man remember about some sixteen-year-old's coochie unless he's *still* getting some?" Trina points her finger. "And Cherise, what do you care about some poontang exercises for? A dildo and a tongue don't care how big it is."

"Whew!" I insert, trying not laugh, but also trying not to get tempers rising again. "Let's not argue and break the mood of the book. Cherise, go on. You read beautifully, you know." I say, attempting to smooth things over again

"Thank you." Cherise replies while starring daggers at Trina. "Let me see where I was. Alright..."

•

The concert is held in an outdoor amphitheater built in the corner of Sessums Park. The area is crowded as we arrive but with luck, we find a parking space not too far from the park entrance. Chance grabs a blanket out the back of the Mustang and we meander through the crowd until we locate a suitable spot where we could see the action, but not be overwhelmed by the sound system.

The concert was really quite good. Hearing the blues music brought back memories of home and I momentarily felt the pull of homesickness. I banish the thoughts beginning to dampen my mood and settle into Chance's chest, determined to enjoy the remainder of the concert.

As the event draws to a close, I find myself famished. After collecting the blankets and moving with the crowd towards the parking lot, Chance suggests we get a bite to eat. The traffic was heavy, but moved quickly and we found ourselves at a Chinese buffet within half an hour.

The wide variety of foods available made me load up plate after plate until I felt full. Chance and I wobbled to the car, overly satiated, after an hour. As he settles into the car, he looks at me slowly and says, "Later?"

I grin. "It's *definitely* later."

Arriving at the apartment complex, I exit the car and rapidly head for the stairwell leading to my apartment. Chance's hands, however, pull and stop me.

"I've seen yours, now don't you want to see mine?" He asks with a grin.

"Right now?" I ask, anticipation of sexual Olympics flooding my brain.

"Yes," he says and stands there with a foolish grin on his face.

"Ok." I turn towards the stairwell again and *again* he stops me. I turn back. Chance remains standing there, smiling at me.

What is he waiting on?

A sudden, wild thought pops into my head. *I know he isn't going to expose himself in the parking lot!* I'm starting to like being adventurous, but not *that* adventurous. I feel an unknown panic starting in my chest.

I know he isn't going to do this right now, is he?! But, he is just standing there, not moving towards my apartment or anything. I look around wildly. Maybe I had misjudged this guy after all.

Chance stares at me strangely and says, "What? Are you afraid to see my apartment or something?"

Apartment? I thought he was talking about whipping it out in the parking lot for me to see and he just wants me to go to his apartment. I laugh in amazement at the crazy thoughts which had flitted through my mind.

"Of course, I want to see your apartment," I say, trying to play it off.

"Oh. For a minute there you were looking at me like I had three heads and one of them was gonna eat you."

I lean closer to him, now my fears have been allayed, and whisper, "One of them is."

This statement must have set the pot to boiling because Chance takes off towards his apartment building like a light, pulling me along behind him. Realizing how this might look to anybody passing, I tell him, "Chance slow down. It looks like you are trying to kidnap me or something."

"I am," he replies but he slows his pace a notch. An imperceptible notch.

We walk quickly up the stairwell and to his apartment. Since I had never been in this building before, I am curious to see if his apartment is identical to mine.

Chance's apartment is lushly furnished in a masculine, Contemporary style. Glass, chrome and leather dominate the living room and large kitchen. Columns divide the sunken living and dining area.

Whoever his interior designer was did a great job.

My thoughts are interrupted as I feel the zipper of my dress being pulled downwards. I turn into his arms and open my lips to meet his smoldering mouth. The dress slides down my legs to pool at my feet and I'm left in only my thongs and sandals. I reciprocate and pull the shirt over his head and open and slide his shorts down his legs. He turns me around slowly, his breath catching as he stares at my gold-dusted cheeks.

"Girl, I want you." His hands grab my waist and pull me into his rising member.

"What are you waiting on, then?" I bait him, my arms encircling his neck.

Chance leans me forward onto a column. Teeth nip at my shoulders and arms. My breathing is becoming shallower and shallower as desire permeates my being.

Wanton desire.

A warm tongue lazily trails down my back, licking and sucking. I grip the column tighter as his lips move lower, settling on my cheeks. My leg begins its erratic rocking as I feel fingers placed on my mound. My legs are slowly spread and I feel the scratch of his goatee as his lips gravitate lower on my cheeks.

Chance turns his body around and I spread wider as I feel his tongue part my nether lips and swirl into Eden. I grab his head with one hand and rock my pelvis back and forth, playing a symphony on his tongue. His hands grasp my buttocks; his tongue plunders me unmercifully. I ride his face frantically, needing this and more.

Around and around.

Bumping, grinding and swirling my hips.

Mewling in need. My juices flowing down my legs.

As I continue to assault his mouth, Chance strokes himself before placing protection on his root. Suddenly, he stands and plunges into my needy center, his hips pistoning rhythmically, my body arching to meet every stroke.

Pleasure osmosing to every pore.

Moans flying past my lips without restraint.

As I feel the needles working their way from my feet upwards, Chance cries out and we ride out the tornado of pleasure together. Our fused bodies collapsing onto the tile floor, writhing in a sensual utopia, as wave after wave of completion slams into our bodies; rendering us senseless of time and space...

•

Moments pass when all I am cognizant of is the ticking of the clock on the wall, the rapid thumping of my heart, and Chance's erratic breathing. Fingers gently flow over skin still hot to the touch, slick with sweat.

I lift myself into a sitting position, my legs gaped and splayed over Chance's abdomen. I look at this irresistible hunk of manhood lying before me.

Tamed.

Weakened.

Defenseless.

A feeling of domination makes me feel all-powerful. Sensuous. Aggressive. Unable to resist, I gently begin massaging his thighs, lightly pulling his bush hair. He jumps as I continue stroking upwards, tangling my fingers into his forest. My lips caress his chest, suckling the tight nipples. A sigh escapes. I move downwards to his abdomen, sucking the sunken navel and nipping at his underbelly.

His member lies at half-mast, beckoning for attention to lift itself upwards. I encircle it with my hand, drawing the sac into my embrace. The head stretches skywards and I lean towards it. My tongue flicks lightly over the tip. A sharp intake of breath follows this action. Emboldened, I lick up and down the shaft, my teeth pulling at the hair on his sac.

Hands reach and entangle in my mane, massaging my scalp.

My lips surround the red-tipped lollipop and suck deeply, the musty scent of his body suffusing my senses. The hands in my hair begin pushing gently, urging this body candy further into my oral cavity. As I begin to alternate between sucking and slurping, Chance's pelvis begins to grind upwards meeting each downward stroke of my lips—his head leaned backwards, his mouth spouting encouraging words, propelling me onwards.

As I cup his sac, hands leave my hair and pull at aureoles swollen with desire; my nub, awakened by his response to my actions, is throbbing. Fingers delve at my button, the juices now flowing copiously.

Chance slides three fingers into me and begins to smoothly ravish my Eden. My body responds eagerly. We push, pull, stroke, suck, slurp, grasp and ravish in concert with each other like well-known lovers.

I tighten my hand around the root of his manhood and squeeze. Chance's face contorts and all his movements cease as his climax rumbles past my squeezing fists.

Hot, sticky loving.

Validating my desires.

Vanquishing our needs…

"First her apartment, and now his. They plan to christen everything, don't they?" Cherise giggles.

"If you're gonna do it, you might as well do up the town! Table. Chair. Sofa. Carpet. Fireplace. Pole. It doesn't matter to me My motto is 'leave no surface unsexed!'" Trina laughs.

"It is not!" I tell her.

"Is too!" She retorts.

"Ain't it kind of funny how any little thing can make you want some? A place. A movie. A book. One time, I went to a drive-in movie with first husband and saw *Basic Instincts*. I tell you once we got home, he was pulling my clothes off of me so fast it made my head spin. Then, he took me in the back room and worked me over something *good*. We had the trailer rocking that night!" Travesteen rolls from side to side, smiling at her memory.

"Trailer? All the money your folks got and you lived in a trailer?" Disbelief is written across Cherise's face.

"Yeah. Most of the folks have trailers where I come from. We got one because we didn't want to have to live with our parents waiting to have a house built," Travesteen explains.

"Girl, you ain't never lied about those drive-in shows, though, Trina says. " I went to a porno one once, and me and this dude I was with never even made it back to the *house*. We got our groove on in the back seat of a 1970 Dodge Polare. That sucker had the biggest rear seat I've ever seen! Shit, we could've had an orgy in there if we wanted to."

"Don't make me remember sex in the back seat of a car!" I squeal. "I got my cherry popped in one on my prom night."

"Ladies! We are getting away from the story," Cherise says dryly.

Aren't we, though. "Okay. Okay. Let's all try to focus and stop reminiscing before we miss the whole point," I try to keep a straight face but I wiggle anyway, still thinking about my first sex.

"Admit it, Cherise, you're just mad you hadn't had this much fun." Trina makes a face at her. "You just go on and read with yo' *jealous* butt."

CHAPTER 7

I awaken on strange sheets, in a strange bed, in an unfamiliar room. At first, I'm disoriented, then I remember where I am—Chance's apartment. He must have placed me in the bed after I fell asleep on the floor in the living room.

I look around. The room is as masculine as Chance is. The green walls and black accessories scream MALE!

I hear off-key singing somewhere beyond the closed bedroom door. The singing crescendoing and decrescendoing to no particular rhythm I can discern.

He might look like Isaac Hayes, but he definitely doesn't have his pipes.

Deciding to stop the mad singing, I exit the rumpled bed, rummage in the closet for a robe, and head out the door.

Chance is in the kitchen cooking breakfast. I sneak up behind him and swat him on the rump. He drops the spatula and upsets a glass of juice as he swings around looking wild.

"Girl, don't be sneaking up on me like that!" He exclaims.

"Why you scared? You must not be living right," I reply, as I rest my head on his broad, bare chest.

Chance is wearing only a hip towel, his muscular thighs and firm hips prominently outlined through the rough terry cloth fabric. Yummy.

"What's for breakfast?" I ask into his chest.

Chance leans me away from him. "Let's see. We've got a Western omelet, French toast, fresh fruit and some freshly squeezed grapefruit juice."

"Who are you trying to feed? Somebody else coming?" I laugh as I survey the food on the counter and in the skillet.

"Nope. Just you and me, milady," he replies. "Give me a hand with this food. We'll eat on the terrace."

I juggle the plate of hot omelets and the pitcher of juice, doing my best to negotiate the sunken living room without spilling a drop of food. Chance is close on my heels, holding the platter of fruit and French toast. We arrange the food and make another foray into the kitchen for plates, glasses and eating utensils.

The sun is bright and the air is damp and warm. The terrace area is identical to mine— small enough to hold a table, a couple of chairs and a lounger. An ashtray on a stand is located in the corner, the cigarettes brimming over the sides, threatening to fall at any moment.

"I notice you smoke," I say as I reach for the French toast.

A grimace mars his fine features. "Yeah. I'm trying to quit. I haven't had one cigarette since we've been spending time together and I'm hoping to keep it up."

"Well, you know smoking is bad for your health. It causes..."

"Yeah. Yeah. It causes cancer, chronic lung disease, emphysema, strokes and affect the unborn child."

"Well, at least you're not at risk for the last one, but the other ones are pretty severe."

"Hey! I've heard all the lectures in the world about it. I'm *trying* to quit. I just told you that," he says sarcastically.

"Whoa! I'm just concerned about your health. I'm not riding your back or anything about it."

Chance abruptly shifts his chair backwards, picks up the ashtray from the corner and empties it into the kitchen trash can. Then, he stomps back to the terrace.

"Feel better?" Attitude oozes from him.

"Not really. Just what was that supposed to mean?" I am perturbed at his tone and hasty movements. "You can buy another pack anytime. You *are* old enough."

Suddenly, I didn't feel hungry. We'd had a good weekend so far and today he wants to get an attitude. This just reminded me how little I knew about this man. I draw in a long, calming breath and stare at Chance as he avoids my eyes and looks at the next door apartment building.

"Hey, I'm going to head on over to my apartment," I say, reaching for a grape and standing up from my chair. "There's some things I need to do."

Chance doesn't reply as I walk through the sliding doors. Good. He's not the only one who can get an attitude around here. My feet scratch in the carpet as I stomp with purpose to the bedroom. Grabbing clothes placed neatly on a chair, I force them over my head.

Shit! I cannot locate my thongs!

Irritated to no end, I grab my sandals and shove them onto my feet. As I reenter the living room area, I see Chance hasn't moved from his seat on the terrace. Still staring.

Picking up my purse and keys off the counter, I leave, closing the door a little too forcefully. My stride is long and purposeful as I walk over to my apartment building, a don't-mess-with-me scowl on my face. Thankfully, I see no one as I walk up the stairwell. I fumble with my keys and push the door open.

With anger surging through my body, I walk into the bathroom, strip out of my clothes and stand under the hot spray of the shower. I take longer than necessary, trying to wash any remnants of *that* man off me. Toweling my body dry, I stare at my reflection.

So, what have you got to say for yourself now, girl? What are you so mad about anyway? He's a grown man and if he wants to smoke, so what? You are overreacting here.

"Shutup!" I yell at my reflection.

Who are you suppose to be anyway? His moma?

"Shutup!" I yell again at the wild-eyed reflection in the mirror.

The ringing of the phone silences the voice yelling in my head.

I'll bet it's Chance calling to apologize. Well, I don't want any apology just yet. "Pick up, answering machine!" I yell, still staring at my reflection.

The phone continues to ring and ring, grating on my nerves. I feel a headache beginning to form at the base of my skull. Realizing whoever is calling doesn't plan to give up, I pick up the phone and snarl, "Hell-o!"

"Analisa, where have you been?" my mother says sternly into the phone.

My mood chills instantaneously. "Hey, Moma."

"Analisa Mathers, I have been calling and calling since last night. I was just about to call the police. *Where* have you been?" Moma's tone is severe.

I look at the answering machine. The message number is twenty. Full. No wonder it didn't pick up.

"Uh...I went out with some friends last night," I fumble with the words, annoyed she is making me feel like I am a child with a curfew.

"Oh, now you got friends. Who was it?"

"You don't know them. I just met them recently."

"I know *I* don't know them. Are you just coming in?"

"No, Moma. I got in late and I'm just getting up."

The phone is silent as she ponders this latest statement. One thing about my mother, she always knows when I am lying to her. I brace myself, expecting a serious dressing down.

"Ahem. Just getting up. I called until 11 o'clock my time and I started calling again at 8 o'clock this morning— that's 6 o'clock your time—and nobody answered until now. You know these friends well enough to stay out all night?" She asks pointedly.

"I didn't say I stayed out *all night*. I said out *late*. I didn't check the answering machine when I returned and I didn't hear the phone ringing until now," I reply huffily. I mean, dag, how old does she think I am?

The silence returns. I hear her breathing into the phone, formulating her next battle strategy. A millennium passes before she says, "Ok. You just be careful."

"I will. Moma…why'd you call? Is something wrong?"

"Oh. No, nothings wrong. I just talked to Myra again and I swear, she had completely lost her mind."

"What? She decided not to get married?"

"Oh, she's *still* getting married. That girl came over to the house yesterday with a copy of *Ebony* and said she had found the perfect gown. She wanted me to mail you a copy of the picture so you would know just what she was looking for. Guess what she wanted?"

Knowing Myra's size, is should be a MooMoo. "Ugh, I don't know. What?"

"Do you know my niece showed me a bridal gown made of lace and scarves and had a split nearly up to her cookie?"

"*What!* For who?" I ask, knowing Fashion Fair didn't have *anything* I could imagine Myra wearing.

"For her! And, on top of it, the gown has a *fitted* short skirt *and* a split."

"A fitted short skirt? For Myra?" My face puckered at the image of Myra in a fitted skirt. Seeing her walking down the aisle from the back, ought to look like puppies in a sack, fighting to getting out. *Why* she would want to expose those ham hocks she calls legs, I just don't know.

"Yes! Analisa, it's time for you to call her and advise her. Myra *cannot* look like some cheap floozy on her wedding day! Talk some sense to that girl."

"Moma, just calm down. When people get married, they oftentimes jump from dress to dress until they find 'The One.' I'll call Myra to find out what she really wants and I'll let you know."

"You tell her to stick to something traditional. She's too big to be having all her body hanging out! I don't plan to be up in that church 'shamed in front of everybody!"

"I thought you said she wasn't big, just big-boned."

"She *is* big-boned. It's just...she *has* put on a little weight lately. Oh my goodness! You don't think she's pregnant do you?"

Here we go!

"Moma, I haven't seen Myra in over a year. I have no *idea* if she is pregnant."

"All this rushing to get married suddenly...I'll just bet that gal has gone and got herself knocked up! Let me get off this phone and call over there and ask her."

"Moma! Myra is a grown woman. If she's pregnant, everybody will know in a few months time. No need for you to call her and ask her."

"Now you listen to me, Analisa Mathers. This is a small town and people talk something awful. If that girl is pregnant, she needs to take her butt down to the Justice of Peace and get married. It don't look right for no pregnant girl to be walking down the aisle wearing white and she's already pregnant. You just making a mockery of the whole ceremony if you do that."

"Moma, this is Myra's life. Let her make her own choices. You just be there and do whatever she asks of you."

"Analisa, I'm old-fashioned. That gal isn't going to strut down that aisle with her belly poking out!"

"Her belly already pokes out!" I say, exasperated.

"Yeah, but not for the same reason. I see talking to you is just a waste of my time. You've been gone too long. You seem to have forgotten how folks are around here."

No, I didn't forget a thing. Small towns, oftentimes small minds. No movies or malls or parks to take their minds off of everybody else's business; whispered tales, embellished a little more with each recounting. Facts are *not* to be relied upon.

"I remember," I reply. "Moma, let me call Myra and talk to her about the wedding dress. We don't know if she is pregnant or not and I for one am not going to ask her. So, please, *please* don't call her and show out on the phone. She will tell you in her own good time if she is."

"Well..."

"Moma, let me call her and I'll let you know something as soon as I know something. All right?"

"Analisa....I'm gonna let you handle this, but, if I don't hear from you by tomorrow, I'm gonna call her myself."

"I'll call her right now."

"You got the number?"

"Unless she has changed it, I still have it."

"She has the same one. Ok, then."

"Bye, Moma."

"Bye. Oh, Analisa, happy Labor Day."

"Happy Labor Day to you too, Moma."

"Bye, baby."

"Bye."

In my anger, I'd forgotten all about Labor Day. What am I going to do with myself today? I thought I'd been spending it with Chance, but that seems to be shot to Hades now.

I sit on the bed and stare through the sheers at Chance's balcony. He is still sitting there, seemingly staring at my window. I walk to the window, part the sheers and gaze at him. He gazes back—no emotions showing on his face, no movement other than breathing, noticeable in his body.

First Halmont, now Chance. What is it with you, girl?

I drop the sheers back into place and lay on the bed, pulling the covers over my head. Sleep comes slowly as I relive each moment of the past few days.

Wishing I could do it over.

Missing it even now.

Myra all but forgotten.

"Don't you think she might have been overreacting?" Cherise asks, putting the book down.

"A little. She knew he was a smoker when she first realized who he was...you know, from the balcony and all. I wouldn't have acted like she did," I say.

"You're right. I would have told him to just smoke when I'm not around or go outside or something. I definitely would have just ignored the ashtray and had a good breakfast with him," Travesteen gushes.

"Now, this is what happens in a lot of fast relationships," Trina states, climbing onto her high-horse. "You've rushed in and don't know each other, but you start preaching and getting on your soapbox about this habit or that habit. If you take the time to date first, then you would know whether or not they have problems you don't want to deal with," she finishes.

"You might have a point there, Trina," Cherise says. "Go figure. Trina with a valid point. The world is sure achanging."

"And her mama had a point when she was talking about marriage and how big Myra wants to look like a floozy on her wedding day." Trina purses her lips. "Big as a house and she's trying to get in the latest fashions."

The pot calling the skillet black.

"Well, I've got to agree with her mother on that. You shouldn't look like a sleaze on your wedding day at all," Travesteen points out. "Each time I got married, I always wore a pure...white...dress."

"Four husbands and you wore a white dress each time?" Cherise lifts her eyebrows.

"Yes. What other color do you expect me to wear?" Travesteen inquires like it's a sin to wear something else.

"Ivory. Pink. Blue. Something other than white. Who are you trying to fool? They all knew you weren't anywhere near being a virgin, *especially* after the third husband, so what was the purpose?" Trina snorts.

"I was pure to my husband. We were starting a new life, so white symbolizes the purity I felt in my heart for him and our new marriage." Travesteen folds her hands into her chest.

"I don't know if I would wear white each time. It seems like blasphemy or something. Like you are playing with the whole ceremony," I say.

"Yeah. If I was sitting up in church watching you get married again and you walked down the aisle wearing white, I would be talking about you like a cackling hen," Cherise chuckles.

"You would not. You guys are missing the whole point of the ceremony. It's not for you, it's for the bride and groom. The audience has just been asked to be a part of *our* celebration. What you want or think doesn't matter one iota." Travesteen huffs.

"But, don't you think it should matter?" Cherise pushes her point. "I mean, you're standing up there in white like you're pure as new snow but in reality, you're really like...like rode over bus slush."

"Anyway." Travesteen holds up her hand in front of her face. " Let's get back to the story. I need to hear some more suggestions I can use in my bedroom."

"If you can't take the heat, then stop fronting at the wedding." Trina laughs.

"Read, Cherise." I command her.

CHAPTER 8

I awaken in a room overheated from the blistering rays of the sun. A headache is just on the periphery, caused by the heat in the room. I stumble out of the bed, struggling like a dying woman, to reach the thermostat, cranking up the air conditioning. While I wait for the air to cool down, I collapse on the couch, which is now so warm, it feels like a cocoon enveloping me.

As I gaze out through the glare of the sun, I see huge hot-air balloons anchored over the park, bobbing to and fro, like giant teardrops dancing. Kids are running amuck, excited about the balloons, the clowns and the pony rides. The whole Labor Day celebration culminates with a huge firework show planned for later on tonight.

Well, I guess since I've got nothing better to do, I can lay right here and see the festivities from my window.

As I lay there, I ponder for the hundredth time, why I'd said what I said to Chance; why he reacted like he did. Did I really like this guy or was I just using him for my own satisfaction? Who did he think he was anyway acting like that? So what if I commented on his smoking? Smoking *is* bad for his health. And mine too if I'm around him and he continues to smoke. Okay, I don't know him well enough to be telling him how to live his life, but I kind of dig

121

this dude and I don't want him killing himself and me with something so trivial. Get a patch, quit cold turkey, but *don't* get an attitude just because I mentioned his bad habit. Shoot!

Girl, you are not his Moma. Shut up and go with the flow for once in your life!

I *am* going with the flow. I've never met and wanted a man as quickly as I wanted Chance. I mean, this is not love at first sight by any stretch of the imagination. More like intense *lust* at first glance—I saw him, we sparked and hormones took over from there.

Yeah, well look where your hormones have left you—still lonely.

"Shut up!" I yell into the ceiling and flop over onto my stomach, allowing my back to cool off. Just as soon as I arrange myself comfortably, the phone rings.

"Arrrgggh!" Who in the world could be calling? Venetra's still mad, I talked to my mother this morning and Chance doesn't even have my number. I shift over to reach the phone.

"Hello."

"Heyyy, sweetheart. I know we got off on the wrong foot the other day, but hey, I just wanted to say I'm sorry."

Oh no, not Halmont again. I knew I should have let the answering machine pick up.

"Halmont, I don't have anything more to say to you. I would really appreciate if you would stop calling me."

"Aw, baby, don't be like that. Girl, I'm the man of your dreams, in living color, ready to give you everything you want."

"Let me tell you what I want. I want you to stop calling and coming by. In fact, when you do see me, I won't be offended if you don't speak."

"See, that's what I'm talking about—your hard attitude. It's no wonder you couldn't keep a fine specimen like myself."

The nerve of this guy! "Halmont, I'm getting off the phone and—"

"Girl, if you hang up this phone, I'm gonna harass you and stalk—"

BLAM!

I cut him off slap in the middle of his sentence. I don't have time for no man drama.

RRRIIINNNGGGG!

"Yes?"

"Girl, I know you didn't mean to hang up on me because *I know*—"

BLAM!

If that ignoramus calls back one more time, I'm calling the police and having my phone tapped. Shoot! Why did he have to call and piss me off after the way my day has gone?

"That's right! Show his ass to the curb!" Trina yells, interrupting the flow. "Y'all see what I mean about those kind of men? A little pimp slapping goes a long way with those type of jokers."

"All of them aren't like that, but you might right about Halmont," I agree.

"I know I am," Trina harumps. "Go on, Cherise."

I fall back on the couch and settle myself between the pillows. On second thought, I take the phone off the hook. That way, I know he won't be calling me.

As I stare out the window again, I hear a quiet tapping on my door. Deciding to ignore it, I switch on the television. The tapping becomes louder knocking, which becomes more and more insistent as I continue to ignore it.

See who it is. Afterall, if it's Halmont, he can't get in unless you open the door.

"Analisa? Analisa, it's Chance. Baby, please open the door," Chance says over the noise.

"Go away!" I yell back at the door. I'm not ready for any apologizing just yet.

"Analisa. Let me in. I just want to talk to you," Chance responds.

I click off the television and walk to the door. "Well, I don't want to talk. Go away and have a good life!" I say and walk back towards the couch.

"Wait! Analisa, I want to apologize for the way I acted this morning. I...uh...I.." Chance stops midsentence and I hear giggling and muffled talking. "Uhm, baby please let me in...uh...people are staring at me and all." Again I hear giggling and talking.

Staring at him?

I glance through the peephole and see Chance standing in front of my door speaking to someone out of my range of vision. He straightens up and I see a child walk past him quickly, staring and giving him plenty of space.

What in the world is going on?

With curiosity scratching at my scalp—and against my better judgment —I decide to open the door. I grab my cell phone off the coffee table and say, "Chance, I'm going to open the door. But I should tell you, I have dialed 911 on my cell phone and if you have anyone with you or if you try any funny stuff, I'm going to push the Send button. The police will be here in a flash."

"She doesn't know anything about the police, does she?" Cherise asks absentmindedly.

"That's fine. I just want to talk. I promise." I can see the contrition on his face.

I hold the cell phone high with my thumb on the Send button as I slowly unlock the door and swing it wide. Chance smiles when he sees me, then glances at the cell phone held up in the air and starts laughing.

"You weren't kidding were you?"

"Don't forget the last man who came over here. Let's just say I learn quickly."

"That you do," he says and hitches his eyebrows at me. "May I come in?"

"Sure." I step back and allow him entry. Closing the door, I say, "You were saying—" I stop as my eyes take in his appearance. Chance has on a Stetson hat, a long overcoat and boots. I can see his bare legs.

Is this joker about to go psycho on me?

"Ah, Chance, what's…ah what's…going on here?" I ask with trepidation.

"What?" He looks at me innocently.

I gesture with my hands. "The hat, the coat, boots, what up with the outfit?" I grip the phone. Whatever he might have planned, I can push the Send button a lot faster than he can get to me.

"I'll tell you in a minute. You like Prince?" Chance says and walks over to the stereo.

"Prince?" I ask, confused by this change in conversation. "Prince *who*?"

"You know. The singer, Prince? Also known as The Artist?" He says, as he glances at me, takes a CD from his pocket and places it on the player.

"Yeah, I like him. Now, Chance, let's get back to the coat and boot thing. What's going on?"

Chance straightens up and turns so quickly, I take a scared hop backwards, my body tensed for flight.

As the music of *Private Joy* begins playing, Chance smiles and says, "*This* is what's going on."

Chance slowly unbuttons his coat, a smile still on his face. As I clutch the phone tighter—ready in case he has a gun under there—Chance flings the flaps wide and I gasp. He has on bikinis, some cowboy boots and...nothing else!

He quickly sheds the coat and I see the bikini is really a G-string with a front pouch. No gun can hide in what I looking at!

"Ohhhhh yes!" Travesteen exclaims and slides to the edge of her chair. "I knew he couldn't stay mad with her for long!"

As I stand there with my mouth open, he begins moving his hips to the beat of the music. Singing along with Prince, he gyrates his hips and punctuates each "Private Joy" with thrusts of his pelvis, causing the pouch—and everything inside—to sling around freely.

"Damn! I wish I was there!" Trina yells.

"Me too!" Travesteen hollers and bounces on the cushions like a bunny on crack.

My body makes a fast recovery from the shock of what I'm seeing. I feel the adrenaline being pushed out by the estrogen suddenly surging through my bloodstream, heading straight for my sexual zones. My head begins bopping to the music. I've never had a man do a striptease for me and I'm kind of digging this scene here. Before I realize it, my body has joined my head bopping to the music. When Chance turns his back and shakes his hips at me, I encourage him with a loud, "Work it, baby, work it!"

"Yeah, work it!" A voice I realize is me, yells. I clutch my hands together and lean forward as Cherise reads on.

Chance turns around, slowly walks towards me and takes my hand. He leads me over to the couch and lightly pushes me onto it. I settle into the couch to watch, the phone all but forgotten in my hands.

Chance throws his hat across the room and rips his G-string off! "You *go* boy!" I yell.

"Ah, sukey now!" Trina shouts, jumping up from her seat and walking around, her arms shaking in anticipation.

Chance does a half split, rises then falls back to the floor. He humps the carpet rhythmically, nearly driving my tense nipples through my shirt. I hop up and began singing with the song. Like a lot of folks, I had no clue as to the true words, but I ad libbed like heck anyway.

"Rudolph Valentino."

Chance lifts his head and rises to his knees as Prince's backup singers repeat his words. Watching him, I feel the tensing of my lower muscles.

"You've got a mind and sense."

"You've got a mind and sense."

Chance crawls on all fours towards the couch, his eyes half-lidded; no smile on his face. My juices are pooling and flowing past engorged lips.

Mine too. I wiggle in an attempt to control the wetness I feel seeping out.

"If anybody asks you."

"If anybody asks you."

Chance reaches my thighs. My hands are immobilized as I stare into his eyes, apprehensive, yet excited about not knowing what's next.

"You belong to— "

"Chance!" He shouts this last part.

My thighs are snapped open and his head plunges between them. Pushing panties aside, I feel his tongue probing and licking my nectar. I moan at this sudden, sensual assault. My hands, now mobile, are roaming all over his head.

His hands grab my thighs and pull me forward on the couch, allowing greater access.

My shorts and panties are stripped away; thighs are placed over muscle-hardened shoulders before he dips his head back into my sweetness. Watching his tongue swirling and lapping almost drives me off the couch. I can't help but cry out as his flicking appendage finds my nub and my legs tremble involuntarily, thighs squeezing his ears; my heels beating erratically on his back.

More and more pressure is applied to my nub and multiple fingers are pushed into my body. I feel myself peaking and my entire body trembles and twitches—spastic and jumpy—as if disconnected from my brain. I climax hard, imprisoning his head in a leg lock as I do a jerky bump and grind on his face…

•

As coherent thought returns, Chance releases his head from the jail I created and smiles. His face and goatee are saturated from my love juices. I place his face in my hands and slowly lick it and his goatee.

"Forgive me?" He asks.

"*Hell* yes!" Trina hollers, her fist pumping into the air.

"Hush!" Travesteen tells her, now on her knees, almost in Cherise's lap as she reads.

"Indeed, I do. Can't you tell?" I say as I lick his lips. I push my tongue into his mouth, tasting me fully. His tongue follows my lead as I swirl around in his mouth.

We finally separate—breathless, chests heaving. Without a word, Chance lifts me and carries me into the bedroom. He lays me onto the bed and reaches over to grab Redman. I smile in spite of myself, knowing whatever he plans to do with Redman…I'm already game.

"Me too!" Travesteen pipes up. "Zay, we've *got* to find this man!"

You ain't never lied!

Chance lays on the bed with his head towards my feet. I watch as he surveys my toes. *I'm sure glad I splurged on that pedicure last week!* Chance takes one toe in his mouth, Redman resting on my sole. The combination of warm, wet mouth and the vibrations of Redman, nearly liquefy me. His tongue slurps and sucks each toe and between. As he begins nibbling on my sole, I start to feel ticklish. I try to retract my foot but he holds it firmly.

"Just go with me, baby. You're gonna really enjoy this," he says over his shoulder. I try to relax my foot and under his skillful lips, all remnants of my laughter dies.

Chance shifts higher on the bed as he moves up my legs. When he does, his manhood is inches away from my head. Pulsing. Winking. A drop of fluid on the tip. I watch this fat red Tootsie Roll grow larger and larger as he moves up towards my knees. I rub my own breasts as I watch his manhood and feel his lips and Redman on my legs.

Everybody leans closer to Cherise. Anticipation, lust and need written all over our faces.

Redman is slowly rubbed over my limbs, from the knees to the juncture of my thighs and no farther. My thighs are spread wide, the suns rays burning my love center. I feel warm breath on my mound hair, but no touch. The anticipation has my muscles knotted up. I try, inconspicuously, to shift my pelvis towards the warm breath to no avail. No touch follows. My body makes movements known since time began in its quest for fulfillment. Just as I'm about to pull my hair out with frustration, Redman is suddenly plunged into my center. A hot tongue follows on Redman's heels, pulling at my taunt nub.

Oh! Oh! Oh! Yesssss!

The sensations overwhelm me, but I still need more. I grab Chance's manhood and quickly stuff it into my wet mouth. "Baby, oh baby," he grunts, as I suck deeply, pulling him backwards into my cavity. He begins to pump Redman rapidly and I keep pace, sucking in time with his thrusts.

"Baby, come here."

I lift my head to see him settling onto his back, his hands motioning for me to come closer.

"Now turn around."

"What are we doing?"

"Baby, hush and sit on my face," he whispers and tugs my hips towards his waiting lips, his mouth covering and entering my Eden without hesitancy. I feel momentarily self-conscious, perched on his face like I am, but his mouth continues to enflame my Eden and I lean forward to claim my lovestick—licking and sucking for all I was worth.

Redman is placed on my button and whatever inhibitions I had, leave as I practically jump up and down on Chance's face, trying to get every inch of his tongue inside of me. His facial hair causing abrasions on my inner thighs; my teeth nipping at his sac.

My movements get fast and jerky. I feel myself wracked with uncontrollable tremors and incredible sensations until finally, blackness fills my eyes, liquid runs down my chest and I feel no more...

"Ohhhhhhhhooooowwww!" Travesteen yells and hugs herself. "Umph, umph, umph, umph, *umph!*"

"Oh baby, youuuuu...you've got what I neeeeddddd." Trina falls to her knees and begins crooning the old Biz Markee song loudly.

"Damn!" I exclaim as I sit there kegeling the hell out of my pelvis. Images of every good lover I've ever had flash before my eyes. Derrick with his ten inches; Terry's thick thighs; Lance's abundantly hairy chest which irritated my nipples just right...Oooohhhh! *Chance, I will kill every one of these heffas if your ass walks through that door! They don't know me!*

"Now, this is some shit I'm gonna do," Cherise says, fanning at her face. "The first time me and my *next* girlfriend have an argument, I'll just put on a thong, shake my money maker and work some shit out!"

"That Chance....damn! Girls...shit! *Chance, ifffff only you knewwwwww."* Trina breaks off and begins singing a Patti LaBelle tune this time.

Travesteen hasn't said another word since her first outburst. She just sits on the couch, eyes closed, hugging herself and rocking from side to side like a mental patient.

"Y'all want to take a break?" Cherise asks a little too perky for me. I can't believe she isn't feeling this like the rest of us are.

"Yeah. And gets some cigarettes, too." I pant, flapping at my chest.

"Cigarettes? Zay, you don't even smoke." Cherise scrunches up her face.

"Girl, after the sex I just had, I need one *bad,*" I deadpan.

Cherise just laughs at this and goes in the kitchen to fix herself a drink. She must have glanced at the clock because she yells back, "It almost one o'clock. Don't you think we should break and go to bed?"

"NO!" We yell back at her in unison.

"If you're tired, take your happy ass to bed! I can read!" Trina shouts, her face a grimace.

"I didn't say I was tired, I was just thinking it was kind of late," Cherise answers as she walks back into the room. "Y'all need a few more minutes?" She smirks.

"Please," Travesteen whispers, eyes closed.

Rhett Butler might have been good to Miss Scarlett, but he ain't never been this good!

We finally float off our individual sex clouds.

"We're ready, I think." I look around at everyone.

Cherise begins again.

CHAPTER 9

I awaken to good food smells. Dusk is settling outside, but I imagine the heat has barely abated. Looking at the bedside clock, I realize I have been asleep nearly two hours.

Suddenly, I hear pots banging punctuated by an exclamation from Chance in Spanish. Deciding to find out what's happening in the kitchen, I roll out of the bed. My fingers brush over thighs and chest still sticky from our earlier lovemaking. Realizing a shower takes a higher priority than whatever is going on in the kitchen, I head for the bathroom. Besides, if something catches fire, the smoke alarm will alert me.

I dash a generous amount of Calgon in the steaming bath water. Turning, I survey myself in the bathroom mirror. My hair is in disarray and red blotches spot my chest, but I feel great. In fact, I want to holler, I feel so great!

I do a couple of deep knee squats to verify to myself how great I feel. On the fifth squat, my knee cracks and gives way. I fall onto the floor, barely escaping hitting my head on the toilet. *So much for feeling great.*

I crawl over to the tub and roll into it, making a huge wake. Water is forced over the sides and halfway across the floor. *Oh good, now Shamu's hair-brained cousin has to clean up the floor too.* I massage my aching knee and lean back in the tub, my breasts floating amongst the bubbles.

I hear Chance walking down the hallway. He peeks around the doorway, a look of concern on his face.

"Don't take another step," I tell him.

"Everything all right?" He asks, looking around the bathroom.

"Yeah, I just had a little spill in the tub."

"You didn't hit your head or anything, did you?" Concern laces his voice.

"No. My head almost played tagged with the toilet, but I missed."

He looks around the bathroom again. "This is some mess we've got to clean up here."

"Yes, it is. What are you cooking?" I ask, submerging my chest into the soapy water.

"Just a little jerk chicken. You ever had any?"

"Nope. I've had fried, baked, broiled and BBQed, no jerk though."

"Good. Hurry up and finish. Foods almost done."

Chance leaves me to attend to the food and I shake my head. *Ain't lust funny?* One minute I'm mad because of the way he acts and the next minute I'm happy because of the way he acts. Go figure.

I ponder the differences of love and lust until the bath water begins cooling. I bend my "trick" knee, testing its ability to bear weight, before I exit the tub. Toweling off, I decide to reciprocate the striptease favor. Since I was so aroused when he did it, I imagine he ought to be just as turned on when I do it. Afterall, turnabout *is* fair play.

Rummaging in my "special" drawer, I locate the item I'm looking for. It's a short red teddy, missing the bra cups and panties. I bought it on a lark, never once really believing I would wear it for anyone but myself. Pulling my robe on over my teddy, I pad into the kitchen.

"Hey, girl, I thought I was going to have to send in the Rescue team to get you out of there. You okay?" Chance asks. He is standing there with only a towel around his hips, the coat, boots and hat resting beside the couch.

"Just fine," I smile and say.

"Good. Sit down. Foods hot and needs someone to eat it."

I sit into the chair and Chance places an aromatic platter of chicken mixed with vegetables and rice on the table. I grab a plate and place a generous portion on it. Tasting it, I say, "Uhm. This is really good. Where in the world did you learn how to cook?"

"From my mother. She always believed in teaching her boys how to cook for themselves. She said she never wanted to send out her sons to be a burden on somebody else. That's a quick way to have them end up back over at her house," Chance finishes with a laugh.

"Thank goodness for your mother. She did a great job."

"That she did," he says with a flourish and a wink.

Chance fills plates with chicken and vegetables and we eat with relish. One thing to be said about lovemaking, it sure makes you hungry. Or is it you are hungry because you forget to eat when you are engaged in good lovemaking? Who cares anyway?

I finish before Chance and I sit watching him enjoy his meal. As he nears the end, I clutch my chest and say, "Ooh, that hurts."

"What is it?" Chance asks, rising from his chair and rushing over to mine.

"My chest," I say pointing to it while closing my eyes and grimacing.

"Let me see."

I peek as he fumbles with the belt and throws the robe open. "Ta Daaa!" I yell, pulling his head to mine.

He pulls his head back, "I thought something was wrong with you."

"Something *is* wrong with me. Can't you see?" I point to my nipples jutting outwards, pointed straight ahead.

"I do see," he says, his head descending towards my chest. I stop him and stand quickly.

"Uh, uh. None of that yet," I say. "Take a sit-down and see what I have for *you*."

Chance smirks and shakes his head, but he dutifully sits down on the nearest chair. I walk over to the stereo and find the CD I'm interested in and place it into the player. I then look over my shoulder.

"I keep on falling iiinnnnnnnnnnnnn loooove, with you." The voice of Alicia Keys suddenly blasts out of the speakers.

A grin splits Chance's lips. I shed the robe, my next-to-nakedness revealed in the dying light of the sun. Doing a slow, steady grind as the song rolls on, I see moisture beading up on his brow. I rub hardened nipples; run my hands up and down my body. I spread my legs wide, squatting (holding onto the couch, of course) revealing the absence of any panty fabric.

"Innnnnnnnnnnnnnnnnnnnnnnnnn. Innnnn nnnnnnnnnnnnn."

I swing my hair around my face as my fingers course up and down my cleft, claiming my moisture; bringing it to his lips.

Chance lunges suddenly, pulling me onto his lap. His teeth claim a long nipple, biting and sucking. I rub my body into his, delighting in his touch.

He reaches underneath me and removes his towel, his member a pulsing being between us. I remove his mouth and fumble in the robe on the floor for protection. Returning, he claims my breast. I slide the protection on, just as he lifts me above his waiting rod.

Staring into my eyes, he slowly lowers me onto him. I feel him glide into me and expand. I try to lift myself for the next stroke, but Chance applies pressure to my shoulders and holds me tightly wedged onto him.

Feeling him.

Twitching.

Throbbing.

Moments pass before he closes his eyes and lifts my hips, allowing me to pump upwards along him. I feel the contractions in his legs as I ride his thighs. He groans with each pump. Hitting a particularly erogenous spot, I increase my pumping action. Chance grabs my waist and begins pistoning into me, allowing me no relief. No escape. My teeth lick his ears and nip at his neck.

BOOOOMMM! Crackle. Crackle. Crackle.

The light from the fireworks illuminates our bodies. I see our silhouettes writhing together on the wall.

Converging.

Separating.

Within moments, my legs begin quivering and I feel the delicious pinpricks of tingles working its way rapidly upward and to my nub. My muscles tighten on his rod and with an anguished "Aaahhhhh!" he throws his head

back and meets me at the peak of the
mountain...

"Now, that's gonna be me!" Cherise stands and claps her
hands.

"Damn! I had a good visual going on and you just messed it
up," Trina wails.

"What?" Cherise asks, perplexed.

"You and that gay shit," Trina says in disgust.

"I didn't say anything about being gay. I just said that was
going to be me." Cherise tells her.

"And you are a female faggot." Trina scrunches up her face.

"Let's just stop this name calling before things get out of
hand." I urge. I don't want to play referee, I want to hear the rest
of the story.

"Well, she started it!" Trina says.

"I did not. You're just mad because you had a brain flash of
getting freaky with a woman. You know your ass just wants to
walk on the wild side and do it." Cherise winks. "Admit it."

"The day I get with a woman, I'm gonna have to be a
paraplegic, no, a quadriplegic and I can't stop the mess!" Trina
flings back. "Get with a woman. *Puh-lease!*"

"Yeah, you want it." Cherise baits her.

"Anybody that knows me knows that I like D.I.C.K. I haven't
had any coochie. I don't *want* any coochie. And I don't plan to
get any coochie, not unless somebody transplants a homo's brain
in this body." Trina thumps her chest.

"Either one of you have the same reaction when I started
talking?" Cherise looks at Travesteen and me. We shake our
heads. "See? You're the only one putting another woman in your
lovemaking."

"And what's that supposed to mean?" Trina bristles.

"It means—" Cherise stands, arms akimbo.

"Nothing. Absolutely nothing. You're not me and I'm not
you. So there." I say, standing between them, cutting her off.

"Yeah, honey, you need to lighten up. You're all the time
ribbing Cherise about being gay and stuff. Why *is* that anyway?"

Travesteen zones in on a question all of us have thought about asking at one time or another.

"Yeah. What is it about my *gayness* that bugs you? It's not like I'm trying to get with you or anything. I'm just over here chilling, enjoying being one of the girls." Cherise shoots off.

Trina stares at all of us hard then, her face...crumbles. One minute, granite, the next, powder. With a flip of her hand, she turns her back and says, "I just don't like gay people. What y'all are doing is wrong. It's just *wrong!*" Her shoulders tremble and we hear a sniff.

What's the matter with her?

We stare blankly at her back, each of us more confused than the other.

A few minutes pass before Travesteen slowly, softly dares to ask, "Trina, did somebody...*molest* you?"

"No. They didn't molest me but...I saw somebody get molested," she finishes between sniffs.

"When! Was it recently?" I ask, surprised at this information. I've known Trina for a few years and not once has she ever mentioned anything like this.

"No, it wasn't recently. It happened when I was a teenager," Trina mumbles.

"It was a...homo*sexual* who did it?" Cherise feels her way slowly.

"Yes. It was a damn homo!" Trina turns and swipes at her eyes.

Shit!

"You want to talk about it?" I want her to talk it out and feel better. Or maybe I want her to talk it out to make *me* feel better.

"Tell us. Maybe then you can get to the root of your fears," Travesteen offers.

Trina begins pacing, not looking in our direction. An uncomfortable silence settles as we watch her. My muscles tense in anxiety as she walks back and forth. Back and forth.

Moments tick by slowly before she inhales deeply and says, "Well, this is what happened. When I was about fifteen or so, my best friend, Betty, and I decided to shoplift a blouse from McRae's. Oh, I wasn't anything like I am now. The part of

140

Jackson where we lived was rough and I was as tough as they come."

Nothing's changed there.

"Anyway, to make a long story short, we were caught and taken to Juvie Hall. They tried to contact our mothers but I guess they were running the streets or with a man or something, so we couldn't find them and tell them where we were." Trina pauses and rubs her forehead hard. "We were placed in a holding cell with a bunch of other girls. Some we knew, others we didn't. We were scared but we were hoping they could find one of our mothers and we'd get out soon."

We nod our understanding.

"That night, after lights were out, this one big girl started pushing up on Betty. Before I knew anything, the other girls had surrounded us and pulled us to the floor. I was kicking and scratching at anything moving. I could hear Betty trying to scream, but they put a hand over her mouth so nobody else could hear."

"Oh Lord!" Travesteen covers her mouth with her hand.

"While they held me down, they tore her clothes off and that big heffa shoved her fist up in Betty. Really *rammed* it over and over and over. The other girls egged her on as the blood began pooling on the floor. I remember wondering if she had some ink in her pocket that was spilling on the floor." Trina laughs self-consciously. "The others just laughed while sitting on my chest. She was still at it when the officers turned on the lights. Her mouth wide open, showing her gunked-up teeth. They had to pull her off to get her to stop." She closes her eyes and is quiet.

God, help her, I pray silently.

"Trina, I'm *so* sorry," Cherise shakes her head, offering an apology that wasn't hers to make.

"What happened to...Betty?" I nervously inquire, knowing she must have needed plenty of therapy after an episode like they'd experienced.

"They took her to the hospital and sewed her up. They let me go with her."

"So, she recovered and got some therapy?" I wish and pray that was how it ended.

"She recovered, but then some of those same girls that helped that big *bitch* decided to spread a bunch of lies about Betty and me. Told folks me and her were trying to dyke everybody in the cell. The lies were laid down so smoothly and they backed each other up, so eventually, folks started thinking we really *were* gay. Even our own mothers." Anger makes her eyes flash.

"That is just terrible!" Travesteen commiserates.

"You telling me. The only people in the world you expect to stick by you and they're working with the enemy." Trina shakes her head. "I just shook the mess off. I didn't care what they said about me, but Betty…she just…couldn't. It just ate at her."

"But she got the therapy and got better, right?" I needed a happy ending to this nightmare.

"No, no therapy. She just took matters in her own hands and slit her wrists when her mama was out one day," Trina states tonelessly.

"*No!*" We all scream together.

"Yeah. Her mother stumbles her drunk ass home to find Betty in the tub with her wrist slit. They say the blood had congealed and the flies were all over her." Trina sits down hard.

Tears flow down all of our faces.

Oh, Trina. Oh, Trina.

"*That's* why I don't like gay people," Trina sums up.

"What did they do to the girl who did this *horrible* thing?" Travesteen squeaks out through her tears. "I hope they sent her away for a long time."

"Naw. She went to a mental institution and was out in six weeks."

"What? You mean to tell me they didn't even send her to jail?" Travesteen howls.

"That's right. The heffa didn't do not one…damn…*day!*" Trina spits out.

"How can that be, Zay? That was a terrible thing she did!" Travesteen looks at me.

"I know, but sometimes…justice isn't served. Look at all the innocent people in jail right now." I wince, struggling for the right words.

142

"Zay, tell the truth. Nothing happened because it was a *gay* crime. They just swept it under the carpet and hoped it would all go away." Cherise narrows her eyes and looks at the ceiling.

"They sure did!" Trina shoots back. "Well, after what happened to Betty, I decided I would have to make a difference in somebody else's life, so I became a lawyer."

"But you're a *divorce* lawyer, not a prosecutor." Travesteen looks confused. "How are you making a difference if you aren't putting them away?"

"When I got out of law school, it was hard to get a rape or sodomy conviction. It still is. They treat the victim way worse than the perpetrator. I decided since most sexual misconduct happens in relationships and since I couldn't convict them, I would definitely make them pay and pay and *pay* their victims." Trina beats her fists on the cushion.

"Trina, I understand you a little better now." Cherise hesitates. "But...but don't judge all gay people by that one incident. We aren't all like that. Most of us are decent, hardworking individuals who want to be with somebody who wants to be with us. The others are just...perverted."

Trina uh hums her, eyes squinted; nostrils flared.

"I agree. That girl may not have been gay at all. It might have been the 'mob' factor which made her act in that fashion." I'm grasping for anything to make some sense of the whole mess.

"Well, I can't and won't speak for that...*monster*, but I do know Cherise isn't anything like that. I think you've been doing her a disservice by treating her like you do. She's *not* that girl! She has been nothing but a real joy to the group. I love her, and if that makes me look gay or a lezzy-lover then that's what you can call me." Travesteen lifts her chin with this last statement and looks at Trina.

I smile at her bravado.

"You need to let the past go and look at the present. You're surrounded by folks that love you and will stand by you," Travesteen finishes, blowing her nose

Trina tents her fingers over the bridge of her nose and sighs. She sits that way for a few agonizing minutes then, looking up, she says, "Cherise, I'm sorry. I don't hate *you*...I guess I just hate what you represent to me and the impact it had on my life. Every since that day, I've avoided anyone I even *thought* was gay. I couldn't stand to be around gay men and I would bristle up at any woman that somebody joked was funny. But...I was wrong to just lump everybody in the same cesspool. I need to judge every one individually, not collectively as a group. I was...sexual profiling and I'm sorry. " Smiling slightly, she continues. " Actually, I kinda like you. Hell! I love you in my own way."

Cherise hops up from her seat and rushes over to her, arms wide.

"Hold up! You're moving too fast!" Trina holds out her arms to stop her.

"Shut up and give me a hug, heffa!" Cherise admonishes her.

"Look, I don't want you to get the wrong idea here," Trina says, before hugging her. "I still think being gay is wrong."

"I know." Cherise looks up at her. "But you've got to admit... that felt *good*, didn't it?"

"Get yo' ass off of me!" Trina yells and pushes her back.

We all fall out laughing.

"Let me read. Otherwise, we'll be here 'til the sun comes up." Trina says, grabbing the manuscript.

CHAPTER 10

The Tuesday after Labor Day dawns foggy. The mist swirls around my windows, engulfing me as I wander onto the terrace. I glance in the direction of Chance's terrace, but I can hardly see more than five feet in front of me.

I relax in my lounge chair to reflect for a few minutes on the events of the past few days. Four days ago, I was feeling alone and lonely. No real friends. No male companions. Today, I've had three *good* days of luxuriating in the arms of a man who awakened urges I didn't know existed within me and buried inhibitions I've held onto way too long.

What a difference four days make!

As scenes of the past few days flash by my brain, my body responds. Sweat lightly coats my forehead, making the fog feel like a cool sauna and I flap the sides of my robe, allowing the cool breeze to chill my skin. My mind plays with the idea of having Redman join me on the terrace, but I discard the notion.

No need to give my neighbors a free, early morning peep show.

I lay back and continue flapping the robe until my body cools. Realizing today was another workday, I reluctantly rise to prepare myself.

•

Driving along the interstate, the sky looks bluer, the air smells fresher, and my spirits are definitely lifted. I honk back at the truckers honking at me, instead of ignoring them as I usually do. I swing into Tylos' parking lot, ready to take on the world.

Ed, the elderly security guard that is a permanent fixture, buzzes me through. "Looking mighty happy today, Ms. Mathers."

"That's because I am." I smile and add a sashay of my hips.

"Well you have a good day for me, too," Ed replies with a lecherous grin he couldn't back up to save his life.

"I'm sure going to try."

As I walk through the foyer and the long corridor to my office, the activity of the place seems to be at an all time high. I see people bustling in and out of offices, speaking rapidly into phone headsets, papers in their arms. I notice a few of my designers with bolts of cloth weighing them down, a harassed look on their faces.

Did I get fired and nobody told me?

I stop to speak with Henries, the administrative assistant. Henries is of Norwegian descent—tall, blond and combative if crossed.

"What's going on? Everybody seems to be running around in a hurry. Anything happen?" I inquire.

Henries places a caller on hold with one manicured fingernail and looks at me over his *Prinz Nez* glasses. "We have got one *big* crisis that exploded in our face about twenty minutes ago. Three of the models for the show got plastered at a party and wrapped their car around a telephone pole."

"Oh, my goodness! Are they—?"

"They're alive, but banged up pretty good. One has a broken leg; one, a broken collarbone and the other one has two beautiful black eyes. So, you realize we can't use any of them for the show."

"Thank God they are alive."

"You're telling me. The downside for us is the only other models we've been able to get *any* type of commitment from are *not* size six— the size of all of the clothes for the show. They are sizes four, eight and ten. We can use the size four, but unless we can find some size 6 models, you will have to remake nearly all of the designs."

"What! The show is in one week! It's going to be nearly impossible to remake almost sixty pieces in seven days!" I exclaim.

"Well, chick, all we've got is seven. This is your first major showing, so you need to decide what and how you need to do this. Mr. Tylos is counting on you. Heck, all of us are counting on you. If the show fails, the orders dry up, profits go down and well... you know the rest," Henries shakes his head.

I wring my hands in frustration at this setback. Sixty suits in seven days would require me working around the clock, using every available hand and then some.

"Hey," Henries says, breaking my revelry, "I hate to sound like the heavy, but times wasting." He pushes the telephone button and begins speaking rapidly into the phone.

I hurry to my office, possible solutions jamming my brain highway. Spotting a junior designer, I ask her to assemble the other three designers for a high priority meeting ASAP.

Before I can drop my purse on my desk, the phone rings.

"Hello."

"Analisa, glad I reached you so quickly," the voice of Wayman Tylos greets me. "Henries tells me he alerted you of our newest development."

"He did."

"Well, any suggestions?"

"I have a few, but I'm meeting with my junior designers in just a few minutes and I will give you detailed breakdown of how we will manage this crisis."

"I'll expect to hear from you within the hour. We don't have any time to waste here. And Analisa, I cannot stress how much we are depending on you and your team."

"I know and you can be assured we won't let you down."

"Neither *you* or *I* can afford for that to happen. I'll talk to you in an hour." Though he didn't come right out and say it, I read the warning between the lines—make this work or you are finished.

While waiting for my designers to arrive, I phone Henries to get a definite answer as to who was committed and what sizes they were. Hearing that so far they had not received any new model commitments, I pull open the design book to begin assembling what materials and supplies I would need for this huge undertaking.

The junior designers—Julie, Maya, Avante and Carol—walk into the office, concern written all over their faces. I quickly brief them on the situation we face. Exasperation, anger, resentment and finally resignation and acceptance was expressed about the dilemma we were in.

After hashing it over for the better part of half an hour, we decide the size four model would wear the bulk of the clothes since we would only have to take in seams and raise the hems. The remainder of the clothes would be equally divided between the new models. Even, so, this still left nearly thirty-five ensembles to remake.

I quickly outline our strategy and present it to Mr. Tylos. He expresses confidence in my abilities and reminds me that he, as well as his wife, were expert tailors and would be available to help. This meant I now had seven pairs of hands versus five.

Leaving his office, I inform Henries that I'll need all the committed models in my office within one hour for measurements and fittings.

While waiting for the models to arrive, the junior designers and I try to determine which ensembles would be the most complicated to remake. The difficult ones, we would resize for the size four; the easier pieces we would remake for the new models. I then delegate who would work on what and contact the warehouse for the materials I would need.

The models arrive promptly within the hour. Though I was not impressed with their looks or attitudes, I kept my comments to myself. My job was to make the clothes hang well on them. The hair stylist, makeup artist and runway choreographer would have to do the rest. After a grueling three-quarters of an hour, in which we measured and remeasured every side of their bodies, I felt confident enough to let them leave. Knowing I would need to have the clothes fitted as we resize and make them, I implore them to keep their schedules open.

By a stroke of luck, Henries arrives and informs me of his success in procuring five additional tailors. They would be expensive, but nowhere *near* as expensive as a "busted" design show. Since they would arrive within two hours, I hurry to rent five additional sewing machines.

Feeling like things were set for the undertaking, I take a breather and rush home for a few changes of clothes and personal items. Having no illusions about the amount of work or the time required to complete it, I gather enough clothes to change at least four times during my stay. Since the executive suite has a full bathroom, I'll be able to shower without coming home, saving plenty of commute time.

I rush out the door weighed down with my supplies, taking care to navigate the stairwell. I was on the freeway before I remember I had forgotten to change the message on my answering machine and place a note on Chance's door letting him know what was going on. I slap my forehead as I realize I didn't even know his phone number. Talk about bad luck!

Reaching Tylos, Ed helps me unload my car and take everything to my office. Seeing the tailors have not yet arrived, I take a moment to try to obtain Chance's phone number through Directory Assistance.

What was his last name? Sam? Simmons? Smith? No, that's not right. Sims? Sims. I believe it was Sims. Chauncey Sims. The operator answers and I ask for the number for Chauncey Sims. She locates the number from the address and I am elated until I received the "This number is unlisted at the customer's request" message.

Great.

Trying the apartment manager was another waste of time. I was told client information was confidential and could not be given out. They'd had problems in the past with unwanted phone calls, stalking, blah, blah, blah. Shoot! I slam the phone down in frustration. I'll just have to break away and let him know what's going on tomorrow maybe. I push all thoughts of him to the back of my mind and focus on the task ahead.

"She should *at least* know the last name of the man she's screwing," Travesteen points out with a frown on her face.

"It was the heat-the-of-the-moment-caught-in-the-passion type of relationship. He did tell her, but like Trina said earlier, she just hadn't had time to learn all the other relevant information yet," I say, feeling the need to defend Analisa's actions since I've been in the same situation myself.

"Yeah, like his phone number." Cherise puts in her two cents.

"She'll get the phone number...eventually," I reply with a chuckle. "Let's go on," I urge Trina.

•

The tailors arrive along with Mr. and Mrs. Tylos. Greeting everyone, I explained how the project would be divided and who would be doing what. Once everyone was certain of their duties, we plunge into the job. Like Henries said, time was wasting.

For five entire days, we cut, sewed and hemmed. The only sleep I got was a catnap here and there when I could no longer focus. I stuck my fingers so many times, by the sixth day, they were puffy and swelling.

As expected, tempers flared, primarily Wayman Tylos', as the deadline got closer. When we put the stitch in the last piece of clothing, I collapse on the sofa, needing a few hours of rest before fitting the models.

The models arrive with the same "prima donna" attitudes. With our already fatigued minds, they frustrated us to the point where I was afraid we would come to blows. But after a private talk with Mr. Tylos, the models return with amazing attitude readjustments.

Nothing like the threat of losing money to give you a better outlook on a situation.

The fitting session finished like a dream. Only one more day to go...

•

The day of the show dawns with us moving like zombies. Mr. and Mrs. Tylos have already left to get themselves ready. Unfortunately, I am on my fourth change of clothes and can change no more. A cup of coffee gives me and my designers a needed burst of energy for the show ahead.

Most people assume the designers are sitting out there watching the fashion show with everyone else. This is not in the least bit true. The designers spend their time behind the scenes, repairing ripped seams, making last minute nips and tucks and fixing hemlines. We work until the last model has walked down the runway.

Pushing myself out of my chair, I am surprised to see Henries walking down the hallway with two police officers in tow.

I wonder what has happened?

I'm shocked when they stop in my doorway. Henries knocks on the door and I motion for them to enter.

"Analisa, ah, these two gentlemen are here to speak with you," Henries states, his eyes flitting to my face then the two men.

The junior designers make a quick exit as I stare at the two men, dreading whatever news they came to deliver. Shutting the door behind the designers, the two men—one, tall and dark featured and the other, shorter and ruddy— flip out police badges.

"Analisa Mathers?" The short one asks.

"Yes. What has happened?" I ask with trepidation.

"Well, we are glad to finally locate you. A Mrs. Estelle Mathers from Mississippi called the precinct this morning and reported you missing. She apparently has been calling your apartment for the past week and hasn't been able to reach you. Since she stated that you had been having some problems with a guy, we decided to look your apartment over. When we checked the apartment, it appeared you hadn't been there for some time so, we got your work address from your apartment manager and decided to see if you were here," he finishes with a smile.

Oh my goodness! I forgot to call and update my mother. Relief floods my body.

I quickly explain the events of the pass few days and my long absence from my apartment. Assuring them I would contact my mother, they leave.

The junior designers run into the office to find out what has happened. I quickly relay the information and quell their fears. We all had a laugh until they begin ribbing me about being a "Mama's baby." I shoo them out of my office and quickly dial my mother's number.

"Hey, Moma, it's me," I say once she answers.

"Analisa Mathers, where in the world have you been? I've been calling you for days and days and I finally decided to call the police this morning. I thought something bad had happened to you! Where have you been?" Moma is not happy.

"I've been at work. We had a major problem with the show. Three of the models got injured and we had to remake nearly all of the clothes in seven days."

"Goodness! I didn't think about calling you there. I was calling at night. I'll bet you are ready to drop. My poor baby."

"Well, I am definitely looking forward to a lot of sleep after this show is over."

"You didn't think to call me and let me know *something*?" I hear the reproach in her voice. "I was scared that Halston fellow had done something *awful* to you. As a matter of fact, I *just* sent your Daddy down to the bank to get the money for a plane ticket. I was going to be out there this afternoon."

"Whoa! No need to do that, I'm fine. Really." The *last* thing I need is for my mother to come for a visit.

"I think I still need to come and check up on you. It's been a while since I've seen you and since I've never been to California, it would be a vacation for me. I'm killing two birds with one stone."

Dread pours over my heart. "Moma, right now I just need some rest. I don't think I would be any real company as tired as I am. I would much rather you came out when I have time to show you the town."

"You don't have to show me the town. I can show myself the town if I want to see it." My mother insists.

"What about Myra? Aren't you still helping her with the wedding and all?"

"Don't mention that girl's *name*." I hear her voice rising. "She tore the sheet with me the other night. Bad enough she wants her back out and her skirt short and fitted, now she wants the dress to be sheer lace with fabric inserts over her 'important areas.' I told that girl she wasn't nothing but a floozy and to get the heck out of my house." I giggle at the vision.

"We don't have girls giving striptease shows at weddings around here. She has to find a better dress if she wants *my baby* to make it or she can just find somebody else to fool with her and her 'hootchie mama' wedding dress."

I can't help myself, I double over laughing at my mother and Myra. "What...what did Myra...*whew*...say when you ...umph...told her that?"

"She told me she thought you would feel it was an honor to make her dress. Then the folks around here could see you really *did* design and make clothes for a living."

"What did you do then?"

"I showed her to the door, aimed the doorknob at the crack in her back and *slammed* it as hard as I could!" I break up all over again. I could hear my mother laughing too.

"Well, I guess that's that."

"And good riddance, too. I'm beginning to believe that girl doesn't have her macaroni fully cooked, if you know what I mean."

"I *definitely* know what you mean."

"Well, baby, you are sounding pretty good, so I think I will postpone my trip until another time. Besides, the fares they charge when you buy at the last minute are higher than giraffe's pus—"

"Mother!" I exclaim, knowing how the line finished.

"Well they *are*."

"Now you can call and cancel and save a bundle." I cross my fingers and hold them to my chest.

"Yes, I guess I can. Let me get off and call and do that right this minute. Call me whenever you get in. OK?"

"I will."

"Love you, baby."

"I love you too, Mama."

"Bye."

"Bye." Yes! I uncross my fingers and hang up the phone.

•

Gathering up last minute supplies, I head over to the Convention Center where the fashion show would be held. When I arrive, music is playing loudly and sporadically. The models are seated in chairs getting their hair and makeup done. Clothing for the show is covered in plastic and lined against a rear wall. Assistants are running around barking orders, changing the lighting, unfolding chairs and checking the catwalk for imperfections which might trip up the models. I settle my things in a corner and lay out a table full of supplies and sat down to wait.

The show goes off without any major hitches. I have to repair only one ripped seam caused by an exuberant assistant doing too many things while trying to zip a model up. One good thing to be said about making clothes at the last minute, you don't have to worry about major weight fluctuations in the models. No chance to gain five or ten new pounds, making the clothes hang differently than expected.

At the end of the show, I collect all of my supplies and high-tail it to the car. There was a post-show celebration party going on, but the way I look and feel, I have no interest in any of it. I tell Henries I would be taking a few days off to recuperate. He gives me a big kiss and shoos me on my way.

I smile when the apartment complex comes into view. Home, sweet, home. I leave everything but my purse and keys in the car and rush up the stairwell to my door. Flinging it open, I head straight for the bathroom and long, hot bath. The bath manages to drug my system and I towel off quickly, giving a brief glance over at Chance's terrace. Not seeing him, I collapse on the bed and pull the covers over my head as sleep claims my body for itself.

"That poor girl." Travesteen commiserates.

"Well, that how it is in the working world. We know you aren't in touch with those type of situations since you've never ever had a job." Trina rolls her eyes above the manuscript.

"What do you mean, I've never had a job? Why, I kept the office for my daddy's chicken farm sometimes, so I do understand about the pressure and working until you're about to fall out." Travesteen thrusts her chin forward.

"Girl, working for your folks ain't no real job. In a *real* job, you've got to be on your game or the next minute they'll be sending you to the house." Trina mimics her chin thrust.

"I know that. Don't think my daddy cut me any slack! I had to be there, on time, just like everybody else," Travesteen bristles.

"Yeah. The only difference is you wouldn't get fired if you were late or decided not to come in at all," Trina replies. "Your cheese was never on the line. You got paid either way."

"I still say a job, whether with your family or not, is *still* a job," Travesteen insists. "There is no difference."

"Hmmmmm. I can't agree with you there," I argue. "If I worked for my dad, he better not even *think* about firing me. I want all the perks and then some. I'm his daughter. That ought to at least give me some extra brownie points."

"I agree, Zay. My parents better never hire me and then try to fire me. That's disloyal," Cherise inserts.

"Yep. It sure would be." I nod.

"See, Steen?" Trina motions at us. "How many hours a week did you work anyway?"

Travesteen scratches at her head. "Oh, maybe ten or so."

"That wasn't no job! That was a hobby!" Cherise chortles.

"Do you even know how many hours in a week is considered full time?" Trina probes.

"Well...ah...ah...yes. It's around fifteen. Or maybe... twenty or so." Travesteen vacillates, her head swinging back at forth between us, looking for confirmation of the correct answer.

"Hooo!" Trina laughs loud. "Did she say fifteen or twenty?"

"Yep. That's what she said., Cherise affirms, nodding her head.

"Y'all stop. She doesn't know," I say before turning to Travesteen. "A full time person is someone who works forty hours a week or more."

"What? Forty hours?" Travesteen says dubiously. "Why that's...that's working all day *long*."

"That's right, Miss America, most folks work eight hours a day, five days a week. Or like you said, all day *long*." Trina smirks.

"Uh uhhhh. I can't see myself working that much each day. I mean, when would I have time to shop and volunteer and have lunch with the girls?" She says, still not believing us.

"You don't. Or you try to fit it in whenever you can," Cherise informs her. "What time was your first appointment with Zay?"

"Four o'clock," Travesteen answers.

"Well, if your appointment was four o'clock, then what time do you think she got there? Two?" Trina asks with a you-uppity-heifer look on her face.

"I don't...know. I never really thought about it." Travesteen shrugs her shoulders.

"Just so you know, I go to work for seven-thirty most mornings and I leave around six most evenings," I tell her.

Comprehension finally dawns. She clasps her hands together and looks at the ceiling. "Lord, *please* don't let me lose my money. I can't work no eight to ten hours a day. Not even for my *daddy!*"

We laugh hard at that last part.

"We've only got another chapter or so left, so let's get back into the story." Trina requests.

"I sure hope they've got some more *sex* in it," Travesteen sighs.

"For your sake, we're hoping the same thing." Cherise pats her leg.

"Chapter eleven..." Trina begins.

CHAPTER 11

"Analiissaaaa. Analiissaaaaa," I hear a deep voice calling, as if through a long tunnel. It sounds near yet, so far. "Analiissaaaaa. I've got something fooorrr youuuu."

Opening my eyes, I realize a dense fog surrounds me. *Where am I?* I look around at my surrounding and see my bedroom, yet not my bedroom. The furniture appears the same, but the room is bathed in a brilliant light. The voice returns, closer, yet still far off.

"Analiissaaaaa. Come and get your pressseeennntt," the voice implores.

Who in the world is that? I wonder. I feel no fear, no apprehension as I wait for the person to reveal himself. The mist parts and I see the outline of a man walking towards me.

"Analiissaaaaa. Don't you want what I haaavvveee?" I hear the man asking. The body comes into view, but the face is still obscured by the mist.

"Who are you?" I ask, feeling a part of this unfolding drama, yet disconnected from it also.

"I've got what you neeeed," the sing song voice says again, the face still not visible.

"What is it I need?"

"What is it you need, you say? Why me, of course!" The face of Halmont—eyes half-lidded, lips shiny, as if from a recent licking—comes into view. He reaches his hand out to grasp me.

"No! No! No!" I scream as I turn and retreat into the fog, sudden fear clutching my heart. "Get away from me! Get away from meeeee..."

My eyes snap open, the last of my scream echoing around the room. I look around and realize I had been dreaming. Only dreaming. Thank goodness!

"I am sick of Halmont!" Trina grunts. "If there was ever a brother needing a greased thirty-eight slug across his ass, it's him."

"Read on!" Travesteen urges.

I groggily shrug the bedcovers off and look around the apartment just in case. Seeing that the door is still securely locked and after searching every room, I return and reclaim my position in the bed. Sleep is not slow in coming...

"Analiisssaaaaa. Come here girl. Times awasting. Analiiisssaaaa," a voice calls to me.

I open my eyes and a dense fog surrounds me. The room is my bedroom, but it is different somehow. Bathed in a brilliant light.

"Analiissaaaaa. Baby, come on. I've got a present for you," the voice calls again, near, yet still far away.

"Who are you?" I ask, a feeling of *déjà vu* prickling my skin. "Show yourself," I say as I swirl around in the mist, trying to get a fix on the direction of the voice.

"Girlllll, I've got what you neeeed. Come and get it," the voice sounds closer, but still I cannot pinpoint the direction of the voice or who it is.

"What is it I need?" I ask and I see a body suddenly revealed in the mist, the face obscured.

"What do you need? Why take a step forward and see for yourself."

Seems like I've heard this or something like this before and I don't feel it turned out right. I take a hurried step backwards.

The body moves forward, the hand outstretched towards me. "I have something for you. Come and get it." The lips come into view. Succulent lips surrounded by a tight goatee.

The lips seem familiar...still, I take a step backwards. The faceless man disappears into the fog. I turn around and around straining to see or hear him.

"Hel-looooo!" I yell.

Silence greets me.

"Heelllllllooooo."

Nothing.

Where is he? Who is he?

"Hell-oooomph!" I say as hard arms encircle me from behind, startling me. I begin to turn to face this man, but his arms tighten around me and hold me firm.

"Relax. It's only me," the voice says in my ear.

"Chance?" I ask. The voice sounds like him but...*not* like him.

"If that's who you want me to be."

What in the world...?

"If you aren't Chance, then who are you?"

"Who says I'm not Chance? Right now, I'm just your dream lover. No names necessary. I can be *anybody* you want me to be. I can do *anything* you want me to do."

I try to turn and face this man, but again I'm held firmly in place. Struggling against the arms holding me, I wiggle and wiggle but gain no leverage. Finally I stop struggling—my chest heaving, my forearms becoming numb from the pressure of his arms.

"What do you want from me?" I ask, dreading the answer.

"I'm not here to hurt you. I come to bring you pleasure. So, it's not what *I* want from you, it's what do *you* want from me?" he speaks into my ear. Hands that held me tight begin massaging my forearms. His chin nuzzles my neck, his tongue flicking at my earlobes. I shiver from the sensations.

"Uhmmm," I moan, as his goatee scratches my cheek. "So you're here to bring me pleasure, you say?"

"That right. Any way, anyhow. The only catch is, you cannot turn and look at me."

"Why not? Is there something wrong with you? You aren't *Halmont* are you?!" This sudden thought makes me squirm again. Futilely, I try to turn my face around to see him.

"No, I'm not Halmont if you don't want me to be. Like I said, I'm whoever you want me to be."

"Then why can't I see you?"

"This is an illusion. A fantasy. My job is to be anybody you desire, to do anything you desire. No more, no less."

"And I can't see you at all?"

"That's the only rule. You can't see me. Think of this as a place with no boundaries, no restrictions, and no inhibitions. What you *think* you want, I can give you. So...what will it be?"

Good gracious. Be with anybody and do anything I want? This is definitely a bomb of a dream. Now, who shall I imagine this man to be? Denzel? Tyree? What about Malik Yoba?

Now there's a man, that Malik Yoba. Hmmm......

But what about Chance?

Shut up. This is my fantasy!

Chance is the man who awakened your dead, tired behind. The one who let the "real you" out the box. Before Chance, you didn't know diddly squat about how good it was between a man and a woman.

I know. Now shut up and let me think. I ponder a few more names—Morgan, Samuel, and Omar...Chance.

Now you on the right track, girl. Chance is something else. He—

Will you please Shut Up! I know Chance. I want this to be somebody I don't know.

I sigh. Since I can't seem to make up my mind, I'm just going to give this unknown man a name. Any name. I ponder for a few more moments. How about...Zeke? Yes, Zeke. I don't know anyone named Zeke, so this ought to be all right.

"Are you ready, Analisa?"

"Yes. I'm going to call you Zeke."

"Zeke, it is. What is it you want Zeke to do to you?" The voice says in my ear.

"I'm...not really...sure. Just get started with the foreplay and let's take it from there."

"As you wish," Zeke says.

Hands which imprisoned me, now rub slowly up my arms and encircle my breasts. Fingers pull at the taunt nipples and I feel the rising of his member into my hips. Zeke's ripe lips nip along my shoulder and lick the base of my neck. My toes curl as his warm breath falls onto my skin. Fingers move down and clench my abdomen as Zeke does a slow rotation into my hips. I arch my back involuntarily, my hands roaming behind me to hold his hips, pulling him closer.

"Lie down on your stomach," Zeke's instructs me.

I fall flat on my face into the soft mattress, my arms and legs spread eagle. I feel the weight of his body as he sits on the mattress. His hands touch my back and I hear a whirring noise. The whirring becomes louder and I feel a warm, soft, vibrating object being placed between my shoulder blades. The object is moved slowly from left to right and to the nape of my hair.

Zeke sits on my hips, the weight of his manhood resting on my lower back.

Feels like he has something to work with!

The vibrating object is laid in the center of my back, and strong fingers begin kneading the muscles of my shoulders. Grasping, circling, kneading. Fingers move down my arms rendering them limp. Minty breath flows onto my cheeks as Zeke's tongue swirls in my ears. Uhmmm.

Zeke's hands move lower on my back. As he shifts downwards, the object is placed at the rise of my hips. Lips kiss the center of my back, following the trail of his hands. I feel my nipples stretching and tensing as his lips move lower.

"Ah...Zeke, so we can do *anything* in this fantasy?"

"There are no barriers to your wants. What you want and desire, I can give you," Zeke's lips return to my back.

"Soooooo, if I say I want another person to join me, is that allowed?"

"Another person?"

"Yes. You know, a...a...*menage a trois*. I've heard about them, so I want to try it."

"Ooooh. Now, I like this!" Travesteen says happily, clapping her hands together like a preschooler.

We look at her but don't say anything.

"What?" She asks, confusion back in her eyes.

"You finished or would you care to elaborate?" Trina asks, holding the manuscript to her chest.

"Just read on," she smiles widely.

> "Okay. Watch this."
> *Can it really be this simple?*
> I see Zeke's hands moving out of the corner of my eyes. The mist in front of me begins moving, taking shape. First the feet, then the thighs. Next, I see the rounded buttocks and the lower back.
> *Those hips sure are plump, not like I really wanted.*
> The back is now being revealed along with a slim neck. Curly hair held together in a ponytail becomes visible.
> *A ponytail? What kind of man is this?*
> "Come," Zeke says. The vision turns and I am stunned to see breasts jutting out from a chest...this is a woman! She slowly walks towards the bed, a smile on lips super-shiny as if gloss was just placed on them.

"She must have written this part just for you, Cherise." Trina winks.

"Shut up, cow," Cherise replies but smiles just the same.

"Wait a minute, Zeke," I say, lifting myself onto my knees. "This isn't what I wanted. I wanted—"

"What? You want a woman more appealing to you?" Zeke asks, as he kisses by neck. The woman walks to the foot of the bed and perches on the edge, lying on her side.

"No! What I had in mind was something *totally* different," I say, watching the woman closely.

If she touches me, I'm gonna scream!

"Like?" Zeke continues.

"Like a man. I want a threesome with two men and one woman—me. Not two women and one man."

"Oh." Zeke suddenly lifts his head from my back. "That is *most* unusual."

"Well, it may be unusual, but this is *my* fantasy and I want a threesome with two men and one woman." I spit out with attitude, hands on my hips.

"Very well." With a twinkle of his finger the woman dissolves back into the mist. "Let try this thing again."

Hands press me back onto the bed; move onto my hips, stroking and kneading.

The mist begins swirling, taking form, first the feet, then the thighs.

My love lips are parted and the vibrating object is placed between them.

I moan as I watch tight slim hips take shape.

Kisses rain onto my cheeks.

A wide back, covered in dark hair quickly follows a slim waist.

Oh yes. My juices stream past the vibrating object.

A wide neck bisected by a straight line of hair is revealed.

The kisses continue down my hips and the object is moved onto the back of my thighs.

A short crop of hair is now evident.

"Come," Zeke lifts his head and says. The body turns towards me and I see the heavy tumescence of his sex, hair flowing from the genitals upward all over the chest. A tight goatee surrounds white, white teeth. It's...*Chance*!

"Yes!" Travesteen screams. "I knew it was going to be Chance. I could tell. This is definitely a love-at-first-sight story. Uhm humm."

We shake our heads at her.

"What are you waiting on, Trina? Go on and read!" She flips her hand.

I told you to include him from the start. Now see who your mind conjured up anyway?

Shut...up!

I smile and lean into his kiss, our tongues stabbing and swirling around each other, my face held in his hands. The kiss deepens and I feel his hands cupping my breast, the nipple trapped between two fingers.

Zeke's flicking tongue replaces the vibrating object, swiping back and forth, slowing parting the lips. The sensation of this slow tongue makes me writhe on the bed; grip Chance tighter.

I blindly pull two pillows down and place them under my lower abdomen, raising my pelvis higher to meet Zeke's lips. Latching onto one of Chance's tight nipples, I suck, nibble and bite, my fingers entwined through his chest hair, abrading the skin beneath.

The sudden scratch of Zeke's facial hair on my inner thighs causes me to bite down hard on Chance's nipple. Chance grasps my face and pushes me farther down towards his abdomen, his hands slowly sliding over my back, rubbing and kneading.

He leans over me and kisses my shoulders and back. I feel his fingers as they reach beneath me and hold the opening to my Eden wide, allowing Zeke's tongue to fill me deeply. I grasp Chance's manhood poised inches from my face. I lick my lips, anticipating wrapping them around him.

A bowl of ice cubes appears magically by my side. I watch as Zeke's hand reaches for an cube then, I hear him sucking it.

What in the world is he going to do with the ice cube?

Will you please at least work *with your fantasy man?!* The voice in my head exclaims.

Hey, but that's not something I've ever really wanted!

You don't know until you try it. Let's give this a shot and if you don't like it, then *tell him to stop,* the voice continues.

Chance takes an ice cube from the bowl and places it into my mouth, his fingers lingering inside my cavity. Zeke's hands resume rubbing my hips and thighs. Suddenly, a cold tongue is plunged between my parted lips.

Oh! Oh!

I suck hard on my cube, my tongue and teeth chilled as they bear the brunt of the cold ice.

Zeke's tongue is rapidly pistoning into me. My cold lips surround Chance's member, a gasp escaping from between clenched teeth. I then feel coldness being pushed inside of me.

The ice cube!

The tongue continues plunging inside of me and I can feel the ice melting, the liquid running from me and onto the pillows. I suck with zeal, pulling Chance into my face.

"Girlfriend is working some things out, ain't she?" Trina guffaws, then resumes reading.

The vibrating object is slid beneath me and onto my nub. I claw into the sheets and gasp for air. Zeke's tongue stops it's magic and I feel its replacement pushing at Eden's door. My hips are grabbed and pulled backwards, releasing my hold on Chance. As I feel Zeke slowly sliding into me, I aid him and forcefully push myself onto his root. I lift myself onto my hands and knees and roughly shove myself backwards and forwards

Filling my channel.

Seeking fulfillment.

Chance slides beneath me, his lips finding my flinging nipples. His hands then grasp them—pulling them forwards as I plunge backward on Zeke.

"Get yours, girl! Get yours!" Travesteen jumps up and down on the cushions.

I don't care what she says, Miss Scarlett has been in this situation before!

"She's getting it! Now be quiet!" Cherise yells.

I grind and circle with abandon, my hand reaching between us to encircle his pumping member. The long, juice-slickened member gliding by my palm; his sac warming the back of my hand.

Zeke throws one leg over my hips. He then lifts me off my knees and gently lowers me back onto my stomach, and slightly onto my side. My upper leg is then raised high and he resumes his fierce pumping. Teeth nip the back of my raised calf and suck the flesh behind my knee.

I feel the vibrating object as it lay in contact with my thigh. I retrieve it and realize it's my old friend, Redman. Handing it to Chance, he turns the setting to it highest level and shoves it onto my throbbing button, his mouth reclaiming my breast.

"Go Redman, go!" Travesteen claps her hands together in glee. "Two men too...*yes*! They got her in a wrangler wrap-up—one in the front and one in the back. Girlfriend knows her way around the bed!" She begins a very *bad* imitation of the Bankhead bounce.

"Ah...when was the last time you said you had some?" Cherise inquires, tilting her head.

"Yeah, when?" Trina chimes in, putting the manuscript down and crossing her arms.

"Forget you stuck-up gals. When the opportunity is right, you've got to *take* it!" Travesteen's hands grab at the air. Then, she stands and shakes her hips, surprising us all. "If I was there, I'd be doing the same thing! You would too."

Scarlett has left the building! Now...who the hell is this?

"Doesn't look like it's been a year, that's for sure." I say, staring at her, trying to see what "being" revealed itself.

"The question that begs to be asked is 'Have you already *been* there?'" Cherise points at her.

"No!" Travesteen abruptly stops her hip shaking. "Why would you ask something like that?"

"You came in here like Miss Celie, now you've turned into Shug," Trina says referring to the characters in *The Color Purple.*

"Am not," Travesteen huffs. "I'm just saying *if* something like this ever were to come my way, I don't plan to sit on the bed acting like I don't want it when I do." Her eyes vacillate between us. Not seeing any buy-in, she sits down and primly folds her hands in her lap. "Besides, it's just a fantasy. I'll never really have the opportunity."

"I don't know...the way you're acting—" I begin.

"Stop it. You know good and well I won't be able to find two men who won't get jealous or something. The closest I'll ever get is in my head." She taps her temple with her index finger.

We stare at her, disbelief clearly evident in our expressions.

"Well, if you do...make sure you come back and tell us about it!" Cherise laughs. "You're rubbing off on me. I think I'm starting to like hearing about other folks sex experiences too!"

"Ain't it good!" Travesteen yells and begins her bad Bankheading again. "Girl, if this ever becomes a movie, I'm gonna buy up all the seats in the theater and take a man and a blow up mattress with me. We *do not* need to be disturbed."

"Not the blow up mattress!" Trina hollers.

"Yep. The biggest, hot pink blow up mattress I can find!" Travesteen hoots.

"I think you better wait for the video or we're gonna be bailing your Southern Belle behind out of the slammer!" I laugh and say.

"Yeah, but think of the stories I'll have for my grandkids," Travesteen says.

"Ah hum. Let me tell them. I can see it now...happy smiling faces looking at there Auntie Trina and then I say...'Your Big Moma was a theater 'ho!'" Trina yells and falls back.

"Girl, you gonna mess those babies up bad!" I laugh. "Theater 'ho."

"Steen, like I said before," Cherise grabs hold of her hands and looks into her face, "buy the video. That way nobody will...ever... *know*." She finishes with a whisper.

"Let go of my damn hand!" Travesteen flings her hands off, a smile playing at the corners of her mouth.

"Zay, get some duct tape 'cause I believe the Scotch tape ain't tough enough for this *heah* closet door." Cherise looks Travesteen up and down, lips pursed.

"You...you think?" I say, trying to catch my breath.

"Let's just...hooooo....get back to the story." Trina says, holding her sides.

The electric jolt I was anticipating did not disappoint. I loudly yell unintelligible words as the vibrations course through me. The sensations making my body shudder and twitch. Zeke grabs my leg tighter in response, his movements jerky and uncontrolled.

Faster and faster we move...

Ping. Clatter. Clatter.

Ping. Clatter. Clatter.

My eyes flip open. I'm in my bedroom and Zeke and Chance are gone.

Ping. Clatter.

What in the world is that?

Ping. Clatter. Clatter.

It sounds like something is hitting my sliding door. As I lift myself from the bed, I dislodge Redman which is firmly placed between my thighs.

Ping.

Is it hailing outside or something?

In my haste, I tangle my feet in the sheets and almost fall. I rush to the door and fling the sheers back to look outside. The sky appears clear.

Ping.

I jump backwards as a pebble hits the door. *What the—?*

I look out over the balcony and see Chance standing on his terrace, a grin splitting his face. He winks and hold up a bottle of wine towards me. I nod an affirmative, hold up my splayed hand and mouth 'five minutes.' He nods back and disappears from view.

I turn from the door and head into the bathroom for a quick shower. My fire has been ignited and I'm hoping Chance can put it out.

"She's gonna put it on him now!" Trina shouts.

"Sure is! She's gonna rock his world after the dream she just had," Cherise says.

"I would too. Shoot, if he was able to get in the room without me raping him, he'd be doing good!" I yell.

"We know." Trina smirks a knowing smirk.

I mellow suddenly at her expression. "What's that supposed to mean?" I ask, a furrow digging into my brow.

"Well...you *are* the one with a bedroom decorated like a whorehouse screw room and with a red door to boot," Trina retorts.

I'm stunned. *No she isn't trying to smear my bedroom! My soul rejuvenator! I cannot let this pass.*

"Now, you might not be able to understand what my room means to me, but don't down it because it's not decorated like yours. I find nothing but comfort and solace in there. It revives me like nothing else does."

"I'll bet." Trina snorts and rolls her eyes heavenward.

What is this heffa trying to say?

"I can't believe you *said* that! All the time I've known you and thought we were tight, you were just thinking I was nothing better than a two dollar whore, weren't you?" I ask, furious with her. "You saw my bedroom and just *assumed* I was an easy lay or something."

"Ignore her, Zay. I always wanted to tell you how brave I thought you were with your bedroom. In fact, I always wanted one like it...but I was too afraid of what other people would say." Travesteen smiles while trying to placate me. "Thirty-eight years old, with a bucket full of money and still worrying about what people would say about me."

"Don't worry about the folks in the street, Steen. Not unless they're throwing some change on the rent or something, that is. Now, Zay, you know how Trina is." Cherise waves offhand in Trina's direction. "She's always gonna down somebody trying or doing something she's scared to do herself."

"I'm not scared to do anything! If I wanted a whorehouse room, I'd put a whorehouse room in my house!" Trina says snidely.

Not liking her tone one bit, I clear my throat before I begin my tongue-lashing. "Well, if any of us should have one, it's *you*!" I yell, pissed as hell. "I never *once* passed judgment on you when you had a new man every other week or when you told me about you and your *married* boss having the quickie in your office—" I hear the rapid intake of breath from Travesteen and Cherise, but I don't care. She wants to try to point the finger at everybody else but her own self, so I'm gonna let the chips fall. She can pick them up wherever they drop. "—and what about the waiter who served us for lunch and you practically *begged* for his phone number? Didn't you say y'all hooked up later on? So, like...I...said...*before*, if any one of us deserves to have a fucking whorehouse bedroom with a fire-engine red door, it's *you*!" I finish, hands on my hips, my neck still rocking.

The tension is palpable in the room. Travesteen's eyes are big as marbles and Cherise is gripping the arms of her chair tightly. Trina is just staring at me.

If she says anything I don't like, I gonna put a pop knot on her head big enough for a goat to suck on it!

Trina opens her mouth to speak and my body tenses, ready to spring at the slightest provocation. Suddenly, she smiles.

"Girl, you are a trip! You know I was just playing with you! I am well aware of what your room means to you. Sheeit! Why you got to put all my business in the street like that? I was just joking," Trina says sheepishly.

"Can't tell." Cherise says drolly, no smile on her face.

"Yeah, Trina, you need to stop playing so much. From the look Zay has on her face, I'd say you were just one step from an all-fire, down-home-country, *ass* whipping." Travesteen retorts.

"Not even a *whole* step," I reply, not ready to accept any apology just yet.

"Zay, get off your high horse. I was just pulling your coattail trying to get a rise out of you. You know I don't think you're an easy lay or anything else you just said. Why would I think that, anyway? I already know the last time you had some, Michael Jackson was still black!" Trina sticks out her tongue.

That one stupid statement makes me burst out in laughter and I feel my anger dissolving.

"Not the last nose job, but when he was black!" Travesteen almost slides out of her seat laughing.

"That was around the same time, wasn't it?" Cherise giggles, then laughs loudly.

"Pretty much!" Trina hoots. "Zay, the only thing that's been up in your coochie lately is Dial and dust."

"Did you say Dial and dust?" Cherise yelps.

"Dial and dust. Only." Trina nods her head, confirming this.

"Stop it! Y'all are just silly as hell tonight," I say, gulping air.

"Probably because it's two-thirty in the morning." Cherise laughs some more.

Trina looks at the clock. "It sure it. Let's finish up this book so we can get some sleep."

"Yeah. I still plan to burn up my American Express at the mall, so let's get through," Travesteen says.

"Okay, back to the story…" Trina begins.

CHAPTER 12

As I am toweling off, I hear a knock at the door. After looking through the peephole, assuring myself it is Chance, I open the door. I am immediately enveloped in a huge hug.

"Analeeesa, you have got some explaiiinnnning to dooooo," Chance says in a bad imitation of Ricky Ricardo.

I laugh and hug him tighter. "You miss me?" I ask.

"Did I miss you?" Chance pulls his head back and look into my eyes. "Girl, for a minute there, I thought you had moved and didn't tell me or something. Then I figured something must have happened and you didn't have a chance to let me know. Where, exactly, *have* you been? I was about to put out an APB on you."

"Don't worry, my mother beat you too it," I laugh and say. "It's been work, work and more work. See?" I hold up my hand to show my swollen fingertips.

"Oh, baby. What happened?" He says as he grabs my hands and begins massaging them.

I give him a brief accounting of what has been happening over the past seven days. Finishing my synopsis, I feel exhausted just remembering all the work.

"Come here," I say, pulling him onto the couch beside me. "What's the champagne for?"

Chance looks at the floor, "Well, I got a big and I mean *big* job promotion. I've been asked to head up a new office of Brown, Inc."

"That's great!" I say and hug him.

"Well, it good in one way and bad in another." Chance lowers his head.

Suddenly concerned, I ask, "What's wrong?"

Taking a deep breath, Chance says, "The job is in Minneapolis, Minnesota."

"Minneapolis?"

"Minnesota." He repeats.

"Why, Minnesota is two thousand miles away from here!" I exclaim.

"I know. I found out right after our last...date. The movers have packed my stuff and I'm all set to get out of here tomorrow."

"No. No. No. He can't leave now!" Travesteen moans. "Not after all the good loving he just had with her!"

"That's how it always is. Bam! Bam! Bam! Then he's out of your life." Trina replies sadly.

"Let's keep on reading. It can't just end like *this*," I say, hoping he really wouldn't leave her when she just found him.

"Yeah, go on," Cherise inputs.

Fear, dread and longing clutch at my body. Chance is leaving. He can't leave, not when we just got to—

You've had a great time, so wish him well and let him go, the voice in my head tells me.

Why? I though we had something here! I silently scream back.

You did, now it's about to be over, so let...him...go.

I continue to war with my conscience, thinking of all the ways he shouldn't go away, leaving me lonely and alone. Again.

I feel his eyes boring into my face, looking for some agreement. Acceptance.

Finally, I realize by expressing *my* fears, I am stopping his progress, his upward mobility. Raising my status in life is the main reason I'm in California, so why shouldn't Minneapolis be the same for him?

With a heavy heart, I reach and hold his face tenderly in my hands. "Chance, I'm so excited for you. Not many people get a shot like this. I wish I could go with you, but I can't, so I'm going to keep these past few days in my heart and in my mind." I kiss him gently.

"Analisa, don't think you can get rid of me so easily." Chance captures my hands. "I've got a gazillion frequent flyer miles piled up and I plan to use every one of them flying back and forth to see you."

"I knew it! I knew he wasn't gonna leave her hanging like that!" I exclaim, happy at the direction the story has taken.

"I'm glad, too. I couldn't bear it if he just walked out of her life, never to be heard from again." Travesteen hugs herself.

"Hush! We're almost at the end," Trina says.

My heart quickens. "So the end is *not* the end?" I inquire, lifting my eyebrows.

"Not by a long hot. That is…not unless you want it to be," Chance says, anxiousness on his face.

I smile, relief and exhilaration flowing through my veins. "I would love to see you, *anytime…anywhere…anyhow,"* I finish with a whisper.

"Baby, I don't know what I'm feeling, but it's too soon for me to want it to stop."

"I'm feeling it too, so….how about you come to my *boudoir* and let's feel it together?"

A kiss gives me my answer. I take Chance's hand and lead toward the bedroom. Happy. Complete.

"Chance?"

"Hhhmm?"

"I've got a fantasy I want to try out and—"

The bedroom door closes and nothing but the sounds of two souls meeting is heard.

THE END

A loud, long "Aahhhhh," in quadruple, reverberates around the room.

"Ohhhh! I hate for it to end," Travesteen oozes.

"Me too," Cherise gushes.

"Zay, I've got to admit I was wrong about this Sydney person. That was pretty good, if I must say so myself." Trina nods her head. "Does she have anymore?"

"Well, she gave me a card…let me get it." I rise to find my purse and the business card.

"Is it cold all the time in Minneapolis?" I hear Travesteen say as I leave the room.

"No. Just in the fall and winter," Trina replies helpfully. "Why?"

"Oh, I just might be *relocating* there soon," Travesteen says smugly.

"I'm going next week. Wanna tag along?" Trina asks.

"You've got a conference or something?" Travesteen inquires.

"Nope. I'm going to see for myself if they have a Brown, Inc. office there and if a Chance Sims works for them," Trina laughs.

"Quit!" I say as I catch the last of her sentence. *Shoot, I'm taking some days off this week, so I'll find out way before you do, sister.* "Here's the card...looks like she has some published already. Wonder why we haven't heard of her before?"

"Let me see." Trina says and grabs the card out of my hand. "SYDNEY MOLARE', AUTHOR OF *Somewhere In America: Situations of XX and XY and Changing Faces, Changing Places,* www.sydneymolare.com. You're right, she already has some in print. I'm going to the website and check it out."

"Give me the information," Cherise says, rising and walking in the kitchen. She returns with a scrap of paper and a pen.

"Write it down for me, too." Travesteen chirps.

"Now aren't you glad we tried out somebody new, Trina?" I rib her.

"Point taken. We will gladly review new authors, especially if they have books like this." Trina taps the manuscript.

"*Especially* if the books cause us to open up and get to the real us." Cherise chirps, looking at Trina.

"It sure did that, didn't it?" I nod, pleased with the way the night has turned out.

"It surely did." Travesteen says, taking her slip of paper from Cherise's hand.

I smile at them. Here we are, having learned way more in one night with the help of one "Small Package" than we knew in the years we've been acquainted with each other.

"Y'all ready to turn in?" I ask, trying to stifle a yawn.

"We'd better if we plan to get any shopping done tomorrow." Travesteen rises from her chair.

"What time should we plan to leave? We know it won't be nine o'clock like usual, so what time?" Trina stands and stretches.

"I say noon." Cherise suggests.

"Cool," I confirm.

"Fine." Travesteen concurs.

"Noon it is!" Trina announces.

"G'nights" are given all around and we go towards our respective bedrooms.

As I open my fire engine-fresh blood-flaming red door, I smile all over again. Walking to the chest in the corner, I rummage around and pull out my own version of Redman—the Pink Panther. Trina might think I'm only getting Dial and dust, but she don't know nothing! Once you go pink, you can hardly think! I guess Analisa is probably is saying, once you go red, you can hardly get out of bed. I giggle quietly. Well, whatever floats your boat.

I hop on the bed and as it begins swaying, I turn the dial to ten...

Here's a Sneak Preview of Sydney's next novel

Grandmama's Mojo *Still* Working

Available Fall 2004

Ode to Madame A

Listen my sisters and hear what I say
Of the words of wisdom from Madame A
Brown as a bean, hips wide as the sea
Words exit her lips stopping the air around thee
Short of stature she stands, but this does deceive
Just ask men snared by her mojo, powerless to leave
Bottle up her essence, sell it on the street
Be the first to get the patent, millionaire within a week
No roots, potions or Ms. Cleo by her side
From years of experience does her knowledge lie
Back unbowed by mind slavery induced by a man
Unenslavement of the mind she preaches wherever she can
Words to inspire, promote, but never demean
Kick him to the curb if he can't treat you like The Queen
Oh the tears that flow from our crying eyes
When we give our all in spite of his obvious lies
One won't act right, another one will
Either way, you'll be breathing still
Flip the script, jump backwards, turn it around
Then you'll be on the road, freedom bound
Disbelieve me if you want, but please hear what I say
"Heed the wise words from Madame A!"

Sydney M.

CHAPTER

1

Exotic?

I stare again at the photo in the book I'd been reading. The caption beneath the picture described this 'perfect' model as six foot one, one hundred ten pounds and exotic looking. Looking at the facial features which strongly resembled an armadillo, I'm convinced that "exotic" is a nice way of saying ugly because this chick is past ugly. She is you-gly! And how many grown women still weigh one hundred ten pounds that don't have a terminal illness? What's wrong with being thick like me?

Disgusted, I toss the book, *The Lane to Personal Perfection,* across the room, barely missing the trashcan I was aiming for. Who writes all these stupid things anyway?

My face scrunches up as I suddenly remembered *why* I was reading the book in the first place. Stefan, my friend—he insists that boyfriend is such an outdated term so we stick to friend—suggested it, along with the others I had been reading for the past two months. He said that the women in these books were the kind he was looking to share the rest of his lie with. Well, I definitely want to be the one he picks. Unfortunately, none of them were even remotely like me.

I'm only a freshman here at Magnolia A & M but Stefan is a *junior*. A fine, sexy junior with curly black hair, light brown eyes, and a bomb of a ride—a 2003 maroon Camaro. We've been seeing each other off and on all semester. More off than on, to be truthful. Things must be changing between us 'cause now he's asked little old me to the big campus Theta ball. A smile splits my lips just thinking how jealous the girls on the hall are going to be when they see him sporting me into that ball...but only if I lose some weight and look like *he* wants me to look.

Stefan has been working on "improving" me since I first arrived. I'm trying to be what he wants...but no matter how I change, it never seems enough. He told me that I needed to update my wardrobe, work on my hair and lose weight, so I did. I spent part of my scholarship money to buy some Tommy Hilfiger shirts—did you know they cost sixty dollars a piece? — got some fake nails, arched my eyebrows but, I drew the line at getting some blue colored contacts. I am *not* Lil' Kim.

Then, I went on the Cabbage diet. Nothing but cabbage, cabbage and more cabbage for fourteen days. I lost ten pounds the first week alone. I tell you I was ecstatic when Stefan started paying more attention to me, but I had to give it up because the gas was killing me *and* my roommate.

I moved on to the All Protein Diet. Now, this diet requires that you eat only meat. It worked too. I lost another ten pounds. Stefan was standing on his head, happy that I was about to become his "dream woman." I was too.

Pretty soon though, my body rebelled. An all-protein diet isn't healthy and my body let me know it. My kidney's hurt from trying to get rid of all the protein waste and I noticed that my sweat was really smelling. Not funky but...I don't know, just *strange*. No matter how many showers I took, I still wasn't smelling fresh.

My roommate told me to get off that fool diet before I killed myself trying to please some boy. Even though I'd lost twenty pounds and Stefan said I was "da bomb," I knew she was right. So, I started eating like every other normal girl in college— anything fast food, fried and of course, Chinese.

The weight was back in a month and Stefan let me know it. He showed out something awful when I began wearing my "pre-weight loss" clothes again. Said I'd just let myself go all to hell. You'd think I was two hundred pounds instead of the one hundred forty I am. At five-four, that's not too bad. Most people think I'm fine...that is except Stefan.

Walking over to the long mirror, I take a moment to survey myself. My skin is clear and chocolate as a Nestle's bar. Black hair, worn any which way I can arrange it to look decent in the morning, just reaches my shoulders. Medium-sized breasts (more than a handful is a waste, so they say) jut from my chest. Healthy thighs connected to a healthier behind complete the package. Turning sideways, I check out the nice protrusion of curvature attached to my lower spine and sigh. I truly have 'junk in my trunk.' *How in the world am I gonna lose twenty pounds in the next two weeks for Stefan?*

Frustrated, I turn from the mirror and fling myself back amongst the clothes on my bed, not caring that I was squishing the navy linen pants suit I wore to the high school awards banquet back in May *and* which I just had cleaned.

The phone rings, interrupting my pity party.

I hurriedly stretch my hand out for the headset. Clearing my throat and swallowing quickly, I lower my voice seductively and say, "Huh-looo." *Never can tell when Stefan would be calling!*

"Sis? That you?" A squeaky male voice says into the phone.

"Weenie?" I ask. Weenie's the pet name for my 16-year-old brother, André Andrews III. He got the nickname from his penchant for hot-dogs. And when I say he like hot-dogs, that's an understatement. He can eat hot-dogs for breakfast, lunch, dinner, snack, brunch, holidays, etc. Shoot, the only thing I know he loves more than hot-dogs is gossip. He likes to hear it and he loves to pass it on, filling in any blanks that may be missing in the original telling, of course.

"Yeah. Whazzup? How's it going?"

"Pretty good. I'm just trying to find something to wear to a ball. What are y'all doing?" I ask as I settle the pillows behind my back while pulling the pantsuit from under my hips.

"Nothing. Shoot, you forgot where we live? What's to do?" Weenie's voice squeals out a high-pitched, shrilly and *familiar* complaint from him. He's always saying he can't wait to finish school, so he can go where the action is. Yokel, Mississippi— population minimus— just doesn't offer that. "Del, did Moma call you?"

I'm instantly on alert. "Ah...no. Is something wrong?"

"Not...really," I hear the hesitation in his voice.

"What's wrong, Weenie?" I sit up in the bed, alarmed.

"Well..." There was a bulk of untold meaning in that one word.

"What?!" I yell, anxiousness and frustration making me irritated that he couldn't just *tell* me.

His voice drops a notch, "Don't say nothing if Moma calls. Just act like you haven't heard a thing from me 'cause you know she like to be the first one—"

"Weenie, *what is it*?!" I cut him off.

"Well, Madame A is in the *hos*pital," Weenie says profoundly.

Madame A is the name our 75-year-old grandmother requested we call her. She said she didn't want to be no Big Moma, Grandmama or Muh'dear. Call her Madame A. 'So dignified sounding,' she told us.

"In the hospital?! What happened?" I ask, as scenes of my grandmother on a life support machine flashes through my mind. I bunch my shirt in my hand and hold it tight to my chest, fearful of what he will tell me next.

"Del, the old girl's still got it. Do you hear me? She's *still* got it! These women walking 'round here trying to be players need to take a lesson or two from that old girl."

What in the world is he talking about? "Weenie, if you don't tell me what happened, I'm going to…"

"Aw'ight. Aw'ight. This is what happened. Madame A, unbeknownst to us and the rest of the town, has two, I said not one, but *two* men friends."

"Stop it." What kind of mess is he talking about? He's got to be exaggerating.

"Girl, she's in a love triangle!"

"Quit lying!"

"I'm not! You 'member Mr. Suge Benson's son by Miz Easter Chaps, Fred?"

"Yeah." Miz Easter Chaps has been Madame A's nemesis for at least a hundred years. I not sure what the whole deal is, but I think it had something to do with her husband and Madame A.

"Well, he's been tipping over to see Madame A on the sly."

"You kidding me?! Mr. Fred's maybe…what…55 at the most! Madame A is *way* too old for him." Now, if he was gonna exaggerate, he could have *at least* made it believable. Ain't no way Madame A was committing cradle robbery like this!

"Apparently not," Weenie says chuckling.

"Yeah, right. Who's supposed to be the other man?" I ask, expecting another unbelievable choice of men in town from him.

"Del, you not gonna believe this here. You know old man Smithey Zacharias that use to run the newspaper?"

"Old *white* man Smithey Zacharias?"

"Yeah, old *white* man Smithey, you know any others?" Weenie says sarcastically.

"Don't you tell me he's the other one?!" I exclaim. I know this *can't* be true!

"Well, he is."

Are they going crazy down there?! Yokel, Mississippi must be about to have a riot!

"Uh uh. What in the world would Madame A be doing with a white man?"

"Now, you need to stop acting like she hadn't opened *that* door before." Weenie says peevishly.

"Yeah, but she wasn't in Yokel. Mr. *Zacharias*? He's got to be all of 70. Are you sure?"

"I don't have no eye-witness account, but they say old girl sure had him cutting up right there on Main Street. So it's safe to say she telling him *something*." I can hear the excitement in Weenie's voice as he relays this tidbit of juicy street trash.

Dog, Madame A's got two boyfriends that seem to be vying for her affections and I can't keep one happy. I couldn't stop myself from laughing, "What happened?" I finally manage to catch my breath and ask.

"Somehow, somebody got their wires crossed and both of the 'men friends' showed up to escort Madame A to brunch on Thursday after her Women's Club meeting."

"O...kay," I say slowly. I don't know what Madame A was doing up in the Women's Club Meeting anyway. She always said they were a bunch of dried-up, old hags trying to run the world like we were still back in "Jubilee" times. Always waiting for "The Man" to make the decisions and we react accordingly.

"Madame A decided that since the mistake was all hers, they should *all* go to brunch together."

"No!" I exclaim. Madame A can't be this bold!

"Yes. Well, neither of these cats knew *jack* about the other one. The way I heard it, they both looked mad, but neither one of them wanted to be the first walk away and let the other one escort her to brunch."

"So, what *happened*?"

"Stop interrupting and I'll tell you! Well, they each had an arm—Mr. Fred pulling her one way and old man Zacharias pulling the other—trying to get her to go towards each one of their cars. I guess whoever got her to ride was supposed to have a leg up on the other one. Anyway, they said they were pulling and pushing on her like an old mule stuck in mud."

"On Madame A?"

"Uh hum. Well, Del, they pulled and pushed until she slipped on a rock and fell flat on her back."

"Oh, no! She didn't break her hip, did she?" I ask with dread, knowing that it took old people a long time to heal broken hips.

"No, she didn't break her hip, but she broke her arm in two places and she has a bruised kidney."

I sigh, disgusted and concerned. "How is she?"

"She's resting pretty good, but Moma is fit to be tied."

"What's new?" My mother, Lena Andrews, is Miss Prissy come alive. She lives in fear that somebody in the family will commit some transgression that will forever shame her.

"She was all scared when Miz June called to tell her they had taken Madame A to the hospital 'cause she fell. But when Moma found out *how* she fell, she showed out something awful at the hospital. Yelled at Madame A and all."

"I can picture that." Moma only worries about *others* transgressing, it's all right when she does it.

"Pissed Madame A off *bad*! Madame A told her and I quote, 'take your dry ass home and don't come back *until* I call for you. Ain't *nobody* asked you to be up in my business.'"

"Ohhhhhh! What did Moma do then?!" I yell. I *know* Lena Andrews didn't take that too well.

"She looked like she was gonna say something smart back, but the look Madame A had on her face must of stopped her. So, Moma snatched her purse off the chair and told me to come on. She didn't say another word until we got home."

"Where is she now?"

"Down there messing up Daddy's dinner yelling and crying about how bad Madame A treats her."

"She know you on the phone?"

"Noooo indeed! She'd take away my Playstation and telephone if she caught me!" Weenie gets quiet, then whispers, "Del, here comes somebody. Bye!" Click.

I place the phone back on the hook and look up at the ceiling. Madame A is a trip! Two men. *Younger* men at that. I laugh thinking about how they must've looked tugging on her and her standing there probably looking cool and collected as usual. The phone rings and breaks my thoughts.

"Huh-loo-ooo." I say in my sexiest hope-its-Stefan-calling voice.

"Delphine Andrews, is this how I taught you to answer the phone?" The stern voice of my mother asks.

I ignore the question. "Hey, Moma, how you doing?"

"Terrible. Things are just a mess. A pure old D mess."

"What's wrong?" I try to interject some surprise in my voice since I already know why she's calling.

"It's your grandmother. She's still running around here acting like she's your age and got her arm broken."

"What happened? Is she all right?"

"What happened is that your grandmother's got man troubles bad. Somebody's gonna get their head cracked open if she don't watch it."

"Man troubles?"

"Yes. Your grandmother has taken up with two men and they got in a tussle over her and she fell and broke her arm. Can you believe this mess? A 75-year-old great-grandmother got men out in the street fighting over her! Main Street at that! It's a wonder somebody didn't get killed!"

"Moma, you sure they were fighting over her? Maybe she got in the way of a fight."

"Yeah, she got in the way, all right. Right in the *middle* of the whole mess. I can hardly hold my head up, I'm so ashamed at her." And the rest of the family too.

"Moma, you overreacting. I'm sure it was just a little misunderstanding and Madame A just happened to get in the middle of it."

"Oh. Now I'm *lying?*"

"No! Moma, I didn't say you were lying at all!" I'd rather *die* than call Lena Andrews a lie. I'll go to *hell* before I do that!

"Sounds like what you said. I tell you that my mother had two men fighting over her and you're saying that's not what happened. I'm here with the action and you're way up there at school and you're saying I didn't see and hear what I saw and heard? Now if that's not calling me a lie, then I don't know what is!" Moma was working herself up something awful!

"I'm sorry. I didn't mean to seem like I was calling you a lie. It's just that...Madame A with men fighting over her in the streets..."

"...is a damn mess! Then both of them showed up at the hospital at the same time. She needs to get them on a schedule. I told her so! Now, she's sitting up in the hospital acting like I did something to her. She talked to me like I was somebody else's child. Who she think gonna take care of her when she comes home? Maynard? Brenda? No! It's gonna be me! That's who." Maynard and Brenda are my mother's siblings. They are constantly at each other about something.

"Moma, just calm down. When's she supposed to get out?"

"The doctor said she should be in there maybe a week."

"Well, we've got Spring Vacation coming up, and since I'll be home, maybe I could stay with her during that time."

"I don't know. Mama can be a real handful. She's so damn hardheaded, I know I'll be pulling my hair out before the first day is through. Let me think about it and I'll let you know."

"That's sounds good."

"Well, baby, I'm gonna go back down and talk with you Daddy. He said he's got a touch of the indigestion. I don't know if it was the hot sausage I messed up and put in the red beans and rice or what. Anyway, let me go check on him. Take care and I'll talk to you soon."

"All right Moma. Love you."

"Love you too. Bye."

Looks like Spring Break going to be a trip!

I hang up the phone with a smile on my lips which is short-lived when I realize that Stefan hasn't called me today.

Not once.

I mentally try to will the phone to ring. When that doesn't work, I scream at it.

Nothing.

Finally, I retrieve the book from the floor and begin reading again. Hey, I've got a long way to go before I reach Stefan's level of perfection and time's wasting.

www.ingramcontent.com/pod-product-compliance
Lightning Source LLC
Chambersburg PA
CBHW031337170626
46807CB00002B/747